Stay Out of the Kitchen!

Stay Out of the Kitchen!

OF THE

A NOVEL

Mable John
AND David Ritz

HARLEM MOON
BROADWAY BOOKS
NEW YORK

PUBLISHED BY HARLEM MOON

Published in the United States by Harlem Moon, an imprint of The Doubleday Broadway Publishing Group, a division of Random House, Inc., New York.
www.harlemmoon.com

HARLEM MOON, BROADWAY BOOKS, and the HARLEM MOON logo, depicting a moon and a woman, are trademarks of Random House, Inc. The figure in the Harlem Moon logo is inspired by a graphic design by Aaron Douglas (1899–1979).

LIBRARY OF CONGRESS CATALOGING-IN-PUBLICATION DATA
John, Mable.
    Stay out of the kitchen! / by Mable John and David Ritz. — 1st ed.
        p. cm.
    1. Women blues musicians—Fiction. 2. African American women evangelists—Fiction. 3. African American women clergy—Fiction. 4. Man-woman relationships—Fiction.
I. Ritz, David. II. Title.
    PS3610.O26S73 2007
    813'.6—dc22

                                            2006102343

978-0-7679-2166-4

FIRST EDITION

146866421

In memory of Ruth Brown,

a friend and an inspiration

Stay Out OF THE Kitchen!

part one

Sanctify Christ as Lord in your hearts, always being
ready to make a defense to everyone who asks you
to give an account for the hope that is in you, yet
with gentleness and reverence.

—I PETER 3:15

Mr. Mario's Downhome Café

The fluffy scrambled eggs, the buttered toast, the crisp bacon and homefries on the side smell mighty good. I'm feeling mighty good being served this beautiful platter of food by Mr. Mario himself. Meanwhile, though, I've got stuff on my mind—my nephew Patrick, a minister in our church, is torn up because he broke up with Naomi, a black woman rabbi he met back when they were both undergraduates at Harvard. And my son, Andre, is about to marry Nina, an actress and model I don't trust.

All this is to explain why Mr. Mario's fluffy eggs, attentive service, and radiant smile mean so much to me. Mario is not a smiling man, but this morning he's happy because I gave him a copy of *Jet* magazine from back in the seventies with him on the cover.

"Lord, have mercy, Albertina," he says, "where in heaven's name did you find this thing?"

"Baby," I reply, "I'm going to pray before this delicious food gets cold. Then I'll tell you. You're always welcome to pray with me."

"Gotta tend to the grill. Give my best regards to that God of yours. Tell him He's doing a helluva job maintaining world peace and harmony among the races."

I ignore Mr. Mario's cynicism—I've known the man for years—and pray. *Father, I just love You, I just worship You, I just thank You*

3

for being the God that You are. I thank You for the chance to relax this morning and reflect on all that is good in my life. Father, You are what is good in my life. I pray for peace, Father, especially for those who have no peace, for those who don't know You, for those who struggle with temptation and doubt. Grant my son, Andre, wisdom and clarity. Grant me the strength to pray for Nina, my daughter-in-law-to-be. May my own prejudices be lifted. Deepen my understanding so that, like Jesus, I can meet people where they are, accept them as they are, love them as they are, and help them as You help me. I pray all this in the precious name of Jesus, Amen.

Just as I'm about to take my first bite of egg, in walks Justine, my forever friend. I can't say I'm thrilled to see her—I was looking forward to a meal by myself—but I'm not about to hurt her by telling her so. Justine's been through a lot lately. I should know. As her next-door neighbor, I hear every detail of her roller-coaster love life. Whoever invented the term "drama queen" was thinking of Justine.

Justine's wearing a large tent dress adorned with drawings of oversized sunflowers. The design makes her look even larger than she is. She seats herself at my table.

"I didn't know you were having breakfast here this morning, Albertina," she says. "How come you didn't invite me to come along?"

"It was a spur-of-the-moment thing, sweetheart," I say. "I didn't know myself until I drove by and decided to stop. I'd been at the hospital visiting parishioners."

"What time you get there?"

"Six a.m."

"That's just about the time I was seeing Johnny Marbee to the door. Have I told you about Johnny?"

"Is he the man who works with you at Target?"

"The very same. And girlfriend, he was sure working with me last night."

I shake my head in wonder. Justine is incorrigible.

4

"Nothing builds up an appetite like some good old-fashioned lovemaking," she says.

"You were talking about a diet last week," I say, changing the subject. I never know what's going to come out of Justine's mouth.

"I'm starting that Palm Beach plan tomorrow. So today is my last day before going to Starvation City."

"What's the Palm Beach plan?" I ask.

"I don't know, but all the Hollywood stars are doing it. It has to work 'cause they have to look good for the movies. I got the book. Gonna read it tonight. After dessert."

I can't help but laugh.

"No laughing matter," says Justine. "Doctor Foster says I got to deal with my weight before it deals with me."

"Baby," I say, "I know it's serious, and I'm behind whatever program you take on. I'm here to help and encourage you. Wasn't laughing *at* you, sugar. I was laughing *with* you."

"Where is that fool Mr. Mario? I'm dying for French toast and a side of bacon. Doesn't that man make a mean French toast?"

"Mr. Mario is the Sam Cooke of the pots and pans," I say. "He's the maestro, and his dad was a chef too. Fact is, his dad also owned a restaurant. He was Italian."

"How long has the Downhome Café been here?"

"He opened up just after he was put off that TV show," I say. "That had to be 1975 'cause I just gave him a copy of *Jet* with him on the cover from 1974 talking about his final episode. I found it at home in an old trunk."

"They're still playing that show in reruns. You'd think he'd have enough money so he wouldn't have to cook."

"Well, that's a long story," I say. "He's never told it to you?"

"I'm not that crazy about the man. I don't ask him any questions. I eat his smothered steak—he can put a hurting on smothered steak—but I don't like him. The man's always angry."

"He got burned bad," I explain.

"In the kitchen?" she asks.

5

"No, by that show. He was the star of the show but never owned a piece of it. He says the producers cheated him bad. Says he could have been a millionaire many times over had they treated him fairly."

"The character he played on the show is the same character he plays up in here. He always has an attitude," says Justine.

"He had an attitude on *Stay Out of the Kitchen* 'cause he was a black cook feeding a family of uptight white folk. That was the humor."

"Didn't they use your song 'Stay Out of the Kitchen' as the theme of the show?"

"They did. I wrote it a little before I wrote 'Sanctified Blues.' But it never made any money till they turned it into a sitcom theme song. Then it made me a whole lot of money. That's when I first met Mr. Mario. He was the only one in the cast who knew the song when it was floating around the bottom of the R&B charts. He loves the old music."

"The brother is light enough to pass. Looks to me like they darkened Mario's skin to make him look blacker on TV."

"They did," I say. "That's another reason he doesn't have good feelings about show business."

"So why does he take it out on his customers?"

"Well, he's sweet to me," I say.

"Everyone's sweet to you, Albertina. You make them that way."

"Sweet Jesus is the one who makes them that way."

"I'm just looking for that sweet French toast. Mr. Mario!" Justine shouts. "Can I put in my order?"

"Hold your horses!" he yells from the grill.

The Downhome Café is a small place, just four booths and a counter, and Mario Pani services it all himself. In my view, Mr. Mario loves cooking and especially loves cooking for his own people. On TV he cooked for unappreciative rich folk. When he was written out of the show, he moved back to this South Central

L.A. neighborhood where his black mother had raised him and decided to do what he likes best.

"See that nasty look Mario just gave me," says Justine. "That man does not know how to treat a customer. He doesn't like his work."

"That's just a façade, baby," I tell her.

"I say he's surly."

"His bark's worse than his bite," I explain.

"I just wanna bite of French toast."

"Have a bite of my potatoes," I offer.

"Don't mind if I do."

A few minutes pass and Mr. Mario still hasn't taken Justine's order.

"This is the last time I'm eating here," she declares. "The man is flat-out rude."

"He's not moving as fast as he usually does," I observe.

"You got *your* food," says Justine. "The man's always been in love with you. I saw that years ago."

"The man has a wife at home."

"As if that makes any difference. Whenever you're in here, he treats you like the Queen Bee."

"Justine," I say, "he treats me that way because of something I shared with him."

"Pastor Merci," she says, "what did you share with Mr. Mario? I know it wasn't your bed."

Justine is just too much, I think to myself.

"No, it wasn't my bed; it was a secret of my heart."

"This is getting interesting, Albertina. Tell all."

Mr. Mario has finally made his way to our table. He's a big man with a handsome moon-shaped face. His hair is white and cut close to his scalp. His beard is also white and neatly trimmed. He stands over six feet and probably weighs close to three hundred pounds. I'd put his age at sixty-five. His nose is broad, his

7

chin square, and his eyes dark brown and intense. His voice is deep and his exacting enunciation the product of the acting school he attended in New York back in the sixties. He told me that he once played Othello in Central Park.

"Justine," he says, "I saw you giving me the evil eye. Now what is it I can make for you?"

"You can make me happy by making me a double order of French toast with a side of bacon. And by acting civilized to your paying customers."

"I am the cornerstone of civilization in this neighborhood, Justine," says Mario, "whether you realize it or not."

"I just want *you* to realize that I'm starving to death," Justine shoots back. "Go cook."

"Make this woman behave, Albertina," he says to me. "Or I'll throw her out on her rusty dusty."

"I'll do my best," I assure him.

The second he's gone, Justine asks, "What's the secret?"

"It's painful."

"Then why haven't I heard it?"

"It's painful to tell it."

"Albertina, you wouldn't have mentioned it if you didn't want to tell it," she insists.

"Sweetheart," I say, "you're probably right. Every time I come to Mr. Mario's I think about it. Maybe that's why I come here. To work out the memory."

"Did something happen here?" Justine asks.

"No, but it happened in a place very much like this in Oakland."

"What happened?"

I pause to breathe deeply. "In a place just like this," I say, "my son Darryl was killed."

"Oh, Albertina, I never knew. You never told me how he died."

"He was shot to death sitting at the counter eating his breakfast just like I'm eating my breakfast. Shot in the back of the head." I pause again, shut my eyes, try to catch my breath. The pain that has never gone away is back in full force. I see Darryl as a baby, Darryl as a toddler, Darryl as a curly-headed ten-year-old hitting a baseball; Darryl going to the movies with his big sister, Laura, and his big brother, Andre; Darryl scared on his first day in junior high, Darryl on his prom date; Darryl drifting away from college, Darryl drifting away from me and his dad and his siblings; Darryl gone for months at a time, Darryl showing up high, Darryl begging for money, Darryl running away from rehab, Darryl lost in the ganglands of San Francisco, Darryl picked up by the cops in Oakland, Darryl jailed and released and jailed again, Darryl not responding to our calls and disappearing when we came to visit him; Darryl's eyes darkening, his eyes filled with tears, his body emaciated, his speech slurred; Darryl showing up in the middle of the night and taking my jewelry from the safe, Darryl weeping as he flees the house, Darryl calling the next day, swearing he'll pay me back, swearing he's okay; Darryl saying how he has a job working in a warehouse, how he has a girlfriend and a place in Oakland not far from Lake Merritt.

And then the call.

It happened in a coffee shop.

Seated at the counter.

The back of his head.

"He owed money," the detective concluded. "These dealers are ruthless. This dealer was sending a message to all his other customers. A public execution is a message that no one can ignore."

"When I first walked by this café," I tell Justine, "I'd see Darryl sitting here at the counter. I'd envision his murder. I'd have to cross the street and hurry away and swear I'd never pass this way again. I'd avoid any café that reminded me of what had happened. I'd avoid eating out altogether. I'd pray to God and then read the

Scripture that says, 'A perfect love casts out all fear.' Perfecting that love meant facing that fear. I read Second Timothy 1:7 that says, 'For God has not given us a spirit of timidity.' My friend from high school, Florence Ginzburg, also urged me to face the fear. Florence is a psychologist with a loving heart. So one morning, my hands shaking, I walked into this place.

"As I said already, I knew Mr. Mario from my show business days. He knew me when I was singing the blues and touring with James Brown. He also knew that I was the one who wrote the song 'Stay Out of the Kitchen.'

" 'I heard you live in the neighborhood, Albertina,' he said. 'I always wondered why you never came in here.' I told him why. The words just poured out of me. As I told the story, I surprised myself by crying like a baby. I knew Mr. Mario, but not well enough to break down and sob right in front of him. You know what he did when he saw me weeping like that?"

"What?" Justine asks.

"He made me the lightest, most delicious cheese omelet I've ever tasted. He made me fresh-squeezed orange juice. He served me fresh coffee with lots of cream. He asked me how many sugars I wanted. I know that sounds silly, Justine, but the way he served me calmed my troubled soul."

"I told you he loves you," she says.

"Yes, but not with a romantic love. It was a love based on compassion. He knew what I had gone through. And the reason he knew was because he had a daughter who had gone through the same thing. Crack killed his daughter before her twenty-fifth birthday. He told me that. And then he told me about his own life. His white Italian American father never married his black mother and left her soon after Mario was born. Mario was named for his father, but they had a strained relationship. Out of guilt, Mario Pani, Senior, sent his son money for college and then acting school. That's where Mr. Mario learned Shakespeare and all the classics. But back in those days, black actors had it rougher than they do today. He might have passed for white but the idea infuriated him. He couldn't find enough work on the legitimate stage to support his family. That's when his father let him apprentice at a restaurant he had opened in New York City. Mario became a cook, and a great one.

"One night a customer was impressed with the meal and wanted to meet the chef. The customer turned out to be a big-time TV producer. That's the man who was starting the show *Stay Out of the Kitchen*. They were looking for someone to play the wise-cracking cook. Mr. Mario fit the bill perfectly. The show never went smoothly because Mario is a proud man. He didn't like the way they wrote his dialogue. He hated being darkened up, thought it was demeaning. He fought with the producers. And after he became the best thing in the show, he demanded more money. But his demands fell on deaf ears and he was fired.

"After that, he was back where he started, scuffling for work that wouldn't come his way. 'I was through with Hollywood, Albertina,' he told me. 'So I took what little money I had, bought me this little place, and told myself I would never again be subject to a white man's whims. Besides, next to acting the thing I love doing most is cooking. I'm a proud black man, and I'm a proud cook. Here I'm king of my castle.'

"He told me that his wife, Blanche, works as a teacher and, between the two of them, they were getting by just fine. His story gave me hope, you see, because he overcame a whole mess of hurt. His story also gave me hope because it took me out of my story. Feeling his pain put my pain in perspective. I could sit in his café and be comfortable. I could even sit at the counter again. With God's help, I could process the pain that I had thought too powerful even to mention. So I started coming here on a regular basis. I think he saw me as the big sister he never had. He knew I was a preacher but respected that I didn't try to shove the Good

Book down his throat. His mother wasn't a believer. She was a militant lady who followed Marcus Garvey. She wanted to live in Africa but never got the chance. She had no interest in God. Mario's just the same. I avoid arguments about God. But in spite of our differences, we have become friends."

"Everyone tells you everything, Albertina," says Justine. "I've been coming here for years and didn't have a clue about any of this stuff. I just thought Mr. Mario was a has-been TV character."

"He's much more than that, Justine. He's a wonderfully talented man with a brilliant mind."

"Then what's he doing making French toast?"

"He's making French toast because he likes serving his people."

"He sure don't act that way."

Mr. Mario arrives with a stack of French toast covered with powdered sugar and crowned with fresh strawberries.

"My dear," he says to Justine, "I hope these comestibles will assuage your anxiety."

"Will you translate what the man's saying," Justine tells me, "while I eat his food."

"Enjoy," says Mr. Mario, managing a small smile. That smile, though, doesn't stay.

The smile turns into a twisted grimace of pain.

His eyes widen.

He grabs his arm, emits a terrible groan, and collapses on the floor.

I run to his side while Justine calls 911 on her cell. Another customer administers mouth-to-mouth resuscitation. Within a few minutes an ambulance arrives and rushes Mr. Mario to the hospital.

The café that brought me peace is now a place of panic. There is blood on the floor because he cut open his head when he fell. The paramedics say he is breathing, but they won't say for how long.

Temple Abraham

Last night's dream was understandably confused. I had just come from a second trip to the hospital. Mr. Mario's heart attack was serious but not fatal. More alarming, though, was the sight of his wife, Blanche. She was in a wheelchair. I didn't know she had lost both her legs to diabetes, and, from what she told me, she also suffered from a kidney ailment. Blanche had been forced to retire from teaching after her amputations. She looked frail and frightened. I asked her if she wanted to pray with me, but, like her husband, she said she had no use for the Lord.

When I got home, I was exhausted. There was a message on the machine from Andre in New York reminding me that his fiancée, Nina, was arriving in L.A. tomorrow and wanted me to help her look for a wedding gown. There were two messages from parishioners requesting private counseling. Bishop Haywood, a friend from Santa Barbara, called to invite me to preach at his church next week. And Clifford Bloom, a jazz disc jockey and Jewish Christian who had become a member of my church, wanted to know whether I wanted to accompany him to see singer Nancy Wilson in concert at the Disney Hall.

I decided to deal with all these questions after a good night's sleep. But the sleep wasn't especially good. A dream disturbed me. The dream involved a murder—it wasn't Darryl, but it was an infant boy—shot on a carousel by a gang of madmen. The madmen turned into dogs and the dogs turned into enormous vultures. I was on the merry-go-round and couldn't get off. The child came back to life but was murdered again, right in front of my eyes. I screamed at the vultures, and they vanished, only to return as ravenous bears.

"Father God," I prayed aloud when I woke up, "soothe my mind and comfort my soul. Fear is the enemy, and the enemy is invading my sleep; the enemy is attacking my peace. But You return me to peace, Father. You shelter me in Your arms. You nurture me with Your love. You are my safe harbor in this sea of crazy thoughts. I know the imagination is crazy, Father, and I know my mind can wander far from You and Your calming heart. Bring me back to that heart, Father. Let me feel Your heart in mine. Let the beat of my heart be the beat of Yours. Let me exchange my life for Yours, my dreams for Yours, my thoughts for Yours. Let me have the mind of Christ, now and forever. In Jesus' name, Amen."

Peace returned.

Now, after coffee and a sweet roll, I'm taking off in my little red PT Cruiser and heading for my ten a.m. meeting with Rabbi Naomi Cohen at Temple Abraham, her congregation off Fairfax Avenue in a Jewish section of the city.

The temple is a modest building built in the forties. Naomi's cozy office, crowded with scholarly tomes, is situated behind the sanctuary. The door is open, and she's working at her computer when I knock softly.

"Good morning," I say.

"Good morning, Pastor Merci. Thank you so much for coming."

"Please, Naomi, call me Albertina."

"Albertina," says Naomi graciously; "I so much wanted to come to your church to have this meeting—etiquette required as much—but I know that Patrick has his office there and . . ."

"I understand, sweetheart. I'm happy for the chance to see you and your lovely office. Looking around, I see we read many of the same books."

Naomi nods and smiles. She has medium-brown skin, dark curly hair in the shape of an Afro, and soft green eyes. She's a beautiful woman whose manner is demure and whose speech is unpretentious. She dresses with quiet style. Her black father is a deacon in an AME church and her mother a white Jewish woman who never practiced her religion. Naomi has told me before that her father was infuriated when Naomi became a rabbi. He wanted her to preach the gospel of Christ.

"Before we start talking," she says, "I just want to emphasize that I don't want my relationship with Patrick—or at least what used to be my relationship with Patrick—to upset the discussions that you and I had."

"Those were great discussions, but, as I remember, Patrick was part of them."

"I haven't heard from Patrick for weeks now, Albertina, and, out of courtesy to him, I don't want to impose."

"Impose in what way, baby?" I ask.

"The idea was to have an exchange between your congregation and mine. I don't want to abandon the idea, but in pursuing our plan, I don't want to give Patrick the impression that I'm pursuing him."

"I understand."

"But will Patrick?" she asks.

"I can't speak for my nephew, sugar. But I suppose there's always a chance of misinterpretation. Sometimes we can even misinterpret our own motives."

"Are you saying that I am, in fact, using this exchange to reach out to Patrick?"

"No, baby, I am not ascribing any motives here. I am saying, though, that the fundamental principle of this exchange is better understanding between Christians and Jews. Seems like that may well apply to your personal situation with Patrick."

"If that's the case, perhaps we should cancel the program."

"And cancel the opportunity to deepen understanding?" I ask.

"I'm afraid . . ." Naomi hesitates. "To be honest, I'm afraid I'm confused."

"Believe me, so is Patrick."

"And your motive is to keep this thing alive?" she asks.

"If by 'thing,' Naomi, you mean this new and wonderful relationship between your worshipers and mine, the answer is yes. Is that what you meant?"

"I'm not sure."

"Look, sweetheart, you have a heart for the Lord. You love the Lord. I feel that with every word you speak. You have black blood running through you, you have Jewish blood running through you, and you've found a way to bridge those cultures and express God's goodness in your life's work. I want you to share that with the people I serve, and I'd love to share my love of God with those who look to you for spiritual guidance."

"And Patrick?" she asks.

I answer, "Patrick will do whatever Patrick does."

The Revelation

The saleslady at the bridal salon at Saks Fifth Avenue in Beverly Hills has a strong Eastern European accent. She's a stout lady with heavy pancake makeup, an elaborate jet-black coif, and a hard-sell approach. These gowns go for up to $10,000, and she's an old pro at moving high-priced merchandise. Her technique is flattery, and my future daughter-in-law Nina does not object to flattery.

Nina is flitting in and out of the dressing room, sometimes in a dramatic gown by Vera Wang or Angel Sanchez, sometimes half-dressed, sometimes barely dressed at all. She is justifiably proud of her body and, given the revealing roles she has played in recent films, she is accustomed to being admired for her anatomical attributes. The saleslady lays it on thick.

"You are a wonder, my dear," she says. "You have an absolutely perfect figure—flat stomach, slender hips, full bosom, and a lovely derrière. You must be a model."

"I *was* a model," Nina confirms. "I'm an actress now."

You're always acting, I say to myself, unhappy with my inability to stop judging this young woman. I pray for a better understanding. I need to understand why my son is enamored of Nina. I have told him that I have doubts about her. Telling him wasn't easy. When a man is infatuated with a woman, not even a mother's warnings can turn him around. In fact, such warnings can do harm. And I'd do anything to avoid harming my son.

"Have you spoken with Andre this week?" Nina asks as she stands before the mirror in a skintight beaded gown designed by Ulla-Maija.

"I have. He sounds happy," I say.

"Ever since he sold his screenplay, he's like a new man. His career has taken off, and we're both thrilled."

The sale of the screenplay for a large sum of money was quickly followed by the announcement of their engagement. He had proposed to her before, but she had put off an answer. Now I couldn't help but see a link between his selling his screenplay and her accepting his proposal.

While she's back in the dressing room dealing with still another gown, a well-dressed man arrives at the salon asking for Nina. She hears his voice and comes running out to greet him. She doesn't mind that she's in her slip. He doesn't mind either. They hug affectionately.

"This is my agent, Jason Farley," she tells me. "Jason, this is my mother-in-law-to-be, Albertina."

I'm no stickler for being introduced as "Pastor Merci," but in this instance it might be appropriate. At the same time, I hold my tongue and simply say, "Nice to meet you, Mr. Farley."

Mr. Farley shakes my hand cordially while saying things I can't understand. After a few seconds, I realize he's not addressing his remarks to me but is speaking into a small device protruding from his ear. The man is on the phone. He completes his call, apologizes, only to have his phone ring again. While he negotiates a deal, Nina's phone rings from the dressing room. She runs back to answer. The saleslady smiles indulgently. "These young people today," she says to me. "Aren't they wonderful?"

I smile and take a seat.

After the calls are over, Nina, still in a slip, confers with Mr.

Farley about an upcoming project. The conversation is intense. Their rapport is equally as intense. With his blond hair and pale blue eyes, Mr. Farley is handsome enough to be an actor himself.

"Sorry," Nina says to me when their discussion breaks off, "but I have to cancel lunch. Jason has set up an interview with a producer who's leaving town tonight. I hope you understand."

"I do," I say.

"And I hope you'll be coming to New York for the bridal shower in May. There's no place like the Waldorf for a shower. It's going to be really elegant."

"I'm sure it will be, dear."

Nina gives me an air kiss and disappears into the dressing room. Mr. Farley gets back on the phone.

I drive over to Cedars-Sinai Hospital to see Mr. Mario. His doctor happens to be at the nurse's station when I arrive.

"Aren't you his pastor?" he asks.

"Actually I'm his friend," I say.

"Well, right now he needs both," the doctor declares.

"Has he taken a turn for the worse?" I ask.

"No, but late last night his wife suffered a fatal stroke."

I close my eyes for a second and call on the Lord. *Father*, I pray, *be with my friend in his hour of need. Let him feel Your strength. Let him feel Your love.*

"Perhaps you can comfort him," says the doctor. "We'll be keeping him here for at least another week. Yesterday I spoke with him about the lifestyle changes required to heal his heart, but right now his pain is far more than physical."

I walk down the hallway to his room. I knock. He bids me enter in a voice which, noticeably weakened, still bears the stamp of an actor. His enunciation is always perfect.

He is lying in the bed, a white gown covering his great girth.

He is attached to tubes and monitors. His eyes are half closed. He looks like a giant beached whale. In soft tones he says, "I presume you have heard about Blanche."

"I have, Mario. And I'm so sorry, I pray that—"

"I know you're a praying woman, Albertina, but I'm in no mood for prayer."

"I realize that. I just came to sit with you."

"That will be a comfort. I know you're a good woman."

"Thank you," I say.

As I sit by the side of his bed, I hear Mario breathe. His breathing is labored, his eyes watery with grief. After a while, I hear him speak these words:

" 'Howl, howl, howl,' " he recites. " 'O, you are men of stones! Had I your tongues and eyes, I'd use them so that heaven's vault should crack. She's gone for ever!' "

Then he recites the same words again, not loudly, but with such passion that his whispers have the force of a hurricane.

" '*Howl, howl, howl. O, you are men of stones! Had I your tongues and eyes, I'd use them so that heaven's vault should crack. She's gone for ever!'* "

Then he stops, his breathing even more labored.

"Would you like some water, Mario?" I ask.

"That's King Lear," he says, ignoring my question. "I always wanted to play Lear. Lear is the role of roles. To imagine his pain, his outrage and confusion, is a supreme challenge. I tried, Albertina, my God, did I try! But I failed. I knew the poetry, I knew the play backwards and forwards, but I couldn't imagine the pain. Now that pain is no longer a question of imagination. It's my reality. My Blanche is gone. So is my life."

His eyes fill with tears. I bring a cup of water to his lips. He sips the water while his tears turn to sobs. I sit beside him and hold his hand. He falls asleep. After an hour or so, I get up and leave.

I'm there the next day, and the day after. He says he derives comfort from my company. My prayers are that he'll find peace. He asks if I would make arrangements for his wife's cremation. His ongoing hospitalization prevents him from doing so. He reminds me that no religious service is to be conducted. I make the arrangements and ask his doctor whether Mario could attend a small gathering of friends in the nondenominational hospital chapel. The doctor says yes. Mario approves the idea. I attend the service and am moved by the testimonies of Blanche's friends. She was much loved. Several of her students speak of her kindness. From a wheelchair, Mario describes his wife, his lifelong companion, as a wise and compassionate woman, a faithful friend whose understanding kept him anchored. "Without her," he says, "nothing will be the same." During the service, the name of the Lord, except in the silence of my mind and my heart, is never uttered.

Later that week Mario undergoes an angioplasty to open the blockage in his arteries and restore good blood flow to his heart. The morning after the procedure, he calls me at home to ask if I'll come to the hospital. I arrive shortly after noon.

Something is very different about him. I've visited enough people after operations to realize that, for a considerable period of time, they are hardly themselves. But this is far beyond the norm. Mario is sitting up in bed. His eyes are clear and focused. His energy is highly charged. My prayer is that, in this trying ordeal, he has softened and sought the Lord. My prayer is not answered.

"I am being transformed, Albertina," he says, "but not in the way you're hoping for. This has nothing to do with your Jesus or His magical blood. This has nothing to do with the superstition of pagan-based religions and the voodoo of human sacrifice. This has to do with food. This has to do with a revelation that has come to me, partly through the words of my doctors but mostly through the death of Blanche. This has to do with negligence. My negligence. My people's negligence. This has to do with my health, and my wife's health. My entire life I have neglected my health and the health of my family, the health of the people for whom I've cooked. My entire life I've been irresponsible. That irresponsibility killed my wife. It nearly killed me. I've been spared, and now I realize why.

"I've been angry. I don't have to tell you that, Albertina. I was angry with my dad my entire life. He was ashamed of me and my mother. Ashamed of having a black woman and a black son. I resented him for that. I hated how, as a classical black actor, I was hit by racism time and again. I was angry with myself for taking my father's offer to apprentice in his restaurant, but I accepted out of practicality. Even at the moment of my greatest success— as a lead actor on a network television show playing an overly educated and erudite cook, making fun of my white patrons—I was angry at the writers for my lousy lines, angry at the producers, angry at the network executives, angry at the circumstances that had brought me into this terrible irony of subservience.

"So what did I do, Albertina? You saw what I did. I picked up my marbles and went home. I simplified my life. I said to Blanche, 'No more. No more officious network execs, no more pontificating producers, no more working for the man.' So I alienated the man to the point where the man could no longer tolerate my presence. Fine, great, wonderful. Let the man push me out. Let him leave me alone. I retreated into a life of simplicity. Blanche would teach. I would cook. I would open my little café and serve the neighborhood where Mama had raised me. To hell with the indignations suffered at the hands of the rich and powerful. During the day I'd cook pancakes and eggs. I'd fry chicken with the best of them. My apple pie could win first prize at any county fair in the country. And on weekends I'd go down to the Watts Center and teach my little Shakespeare class to gifted young people who felt what I felt at an early age—the love of a thunderous language that contains all the poetry of heaven and earth. That was the plan I pursued, Albertina. And for many, many years, my plan worked.

"Except for one thing—for all my supposed brilliance, my plan was not brilliant enough to include thoughts of physical health. Intellectual health, yes. Artistic health, yes. Emotional restraint, yes. I kept myself from going off on people. I kept myself from going off on the world. But in the process, I nearly ate myself to death. And Blanche, who followed my lead, died of diabetes three days before her sixtieth birthday.

"I don't want to wear you out with my ranting, Albertina. Thank you for listening. You are a patient woman. I appreciate that. I can speak to you forthrightly. I've called you here because I need a worthy witness. You are that witness. I know you won't consider me a megalomaniac if I say that I am a man of extravagant charisma. I am a man of force. I'm articulate. I'm learned. People listen to me. When I want to, I can draw a crowd. Well, this wellspring of energy that has been building up inside me, this energy of grief and regret and misdirected purpose is about to explode. But I don't want that explosion to be destructive. I want it to be creative. I want it to be helpful. I want to create a dialogue with my people about health and healthy eating. I want to make amends to myself and Blanche. I want her passing to be an awakening, not a death. I want to go out there and make a difference, Albertina. And I want you to believe that I'm going to do it. It's important that one person I respect believe in my mission. Am I talking like a crazy man?"

"Not at all, Mario."

"And do you believe me?"

"With all my heart, yes."

"Gueϫϫ Who I Saw Today?"

Nancy Wilson is singing her most famous song. I love Nancy, not only because she has let her hair go silver and looks more stunning as a result, but because she's a great and glorious singer with style, flair, and impeccable taste. She's singing a concert tonight.

While Nancy is singing her rendition of "Guess Who I Saw Today?"—which is more a one-act play than a song—I'm seated in the first row next to Clifford Bloom. We have superb seats because Clifford, a jazz deejay, is a friend of Nancy's promoter.

Nancy looks exquisite in a silver beaded gown. She's still slender and her voice still sultry. Sometimes she reminds me of Sarah Vaughan; sometimes she reminds me of Ella. Those are the women that the lady singers of my generation revered and emulated. The blues singers, the pop singers, the jazz singers—we all loved Sarah and Ella and, of course, Billie Holiday. Listening to Nancy, my mind goes back to when I first saw Billie in Detroit. I was nobody then, but a young man named Berry Gordy thought I had something and decided to manage me. He said, "Albertina, go to the Flame Bar and Showroom and watch Billie Holiday. See how it's done."

I went, and Billie, for all her troubles, became my guardian angel for a week. She came early to watch my opening set. "Girl," she said, "you got something of your own. You don't have to imitate me. Mind you, I don't take offense. I'm flattered. But when you sing I want to hear Albertina's story, not Billie's story. Billie's story is too sad for you."

I loved Billie's story because it showed me how pain can turn to triumph. For all her pain, Billie triumphed. She turned her pain to victory. Just like Jesus Christ. In going through His transformation, He showed how we can do the same. Take the hurt, take the unbearable suffering, and find peace, not just for today, but forever. Billie's blues helped me find peace. She helped me find myself. She said, "Go your own way." Finally that way led to embracing God. Without Billie, I'm not sure I would have gotten there.

"The great singers are deep," Clifford Bloom tells me during intermission. "And Nancy is one of the greats."

It's as though Clifford has been reading my mind. That makes me a little uncomfortable. In all ways, Clifford is a gentleman. At seventy-five, he's five years older than I am. At six feet six or seven, he reminds me of my uncle William, the first in our family to go to college. Uncle William had light skin, blue eyes, and a soft speaking voice. Clifford's voice is deep. He can't help it if he always sounds like he's on the air. That's an occupational hazard for all disc jockeys. He also can't restrain himself from showing me how much he knows about jazz, which is a great deal. He tells me how Nancy Wilson was discovered by Cannonball Adderley, how Cannonball played on her first album, and how Capitol Records signed her. He knows the personnel at every one of her recording dates and has a decided opinion about the quality of each. I don't blame Clifford for dispensing this knowledge. It's hard to keep so much information inside. You want to share it.

I have much to share with Clifford. Of all the people I know, he understands more than anyone the relationship between

Nancy and our common mentors—Ella, Sarah, and Billie. Mention Dinah Washington to Clifford and he'll tell half a dozen Dinah stories. And trust me, his Dinah stories are a lot more vivid than mine. Clifford's a great storyteller. He's also an elegant dresser who looks far younger than his years. More than once, he tells me how he works out five days a week. Like many converts to Christianity, his love for the Lord is passionate and comes from a place of great gratitude.

Then why am I uncomfortable?

"Maybe it's because you really like him," Justine tells me the next day when she calls to ask about the date.

"I do like him."

"I mean really, really jump-in-bed like him."

"I'm not jumping in bed with anybody, Justine. You know better than that!"

"That's your problem," she says. "You killed off that part of your life. Then Clifford comes along and you get nervous. You get nervous 'cause the man's sending you vibes."

"I'm too old for vibes," I say.

"We ain't ever too old for vibes. You say he's in great shape. Well, lots of men that age still have that tiger in the tank."

"I'm not talking about sex, Justine—"

"I am. I'm talking about Johnny Marbee, my friend from Target. You talk about a tiger. Girl, this boy's tank is always filled to the brim."

"I'm talking companionship," I say, "and I admit that Clifford is a fine companion. Always a gentleman. And a wonderful conversationalist."

"He take you out to eat?"

"He did."

"Where?"

"La Scala."

"That fancy Italian restaurant in Beverly Hills?"

"Yes."

"Well," says Justine, "the man has money and is willing to spend it on you. Another reason to give up a little loving. Did he make a move?"

"I told you he was a perfect gentleman."

"That just means his move would be smooth. Was it?"

"Justine," I say, "we talked about music all night."

"So you stayed at his place all night?"

"I don't mean 'all night' in that sense. I mean we talked about music *all evening*."

"And when the evening was over, did he suggest you listen to music on the high-priced stereo system at his place?"

"Matter of fact, he did."

"All right, Clifford!" Justine shouts. "I'm liking this boy more and more. I like men who take action. I like it when they out and out ask for it. Did you go?"

"Of course not, baby."

"Were you offended?" asks Justine.

"No, because he put it in a very nice way. There was no pressure. To be honest, I might have even been flattered."

"Those are those vibes I was talking about, Albertina. You do have the vibes."

"He took me home and that was it."

"A kiss on the cheek?"

"Yes," I admit.

"And that felt good?"

"He's sweet. He loves the Lord."

"The Lord ain't gonna protect you."

"The Lord's always protecting me," I say.

"Albertina," says Justine. "You are flat-out impossible!"

Stir-Fry

It's Sunday morning at House of Trust, the old bank building on Adams Boulevard that we converted into a small but sturdy church, and I'm preaching about prayer. I'm telling the congregation of fifty or sixty souls that the key to unlocking the door to the kingdom is prayer. But what is prayer? "Prayer," I say, "is communicating with your maker. Prayer is reaching out to Father God. Prayer is letting your heart speak to Him. And letting Him speak to your heart. Prayer is a way of life that will change your life. Constant, continual prayer means that the door to your heart is always open, and that God doesn't have to knock to come in. God is invited to live inside you. True prayer asks God to dwell within you forever and ever. When Jesus teaches His disciples—and we are His disciples—how to pray in Matthew 6:9, he says to begin with 'Our Father . . .'" He doesn't say 'my Father'; He doesn't say 'your Father'; He says 'our.' We pray individually but we also pray as a community of believers. As a community, our prayer is not simply for ourselves but for each other. As Christ serves us, we serve Him by serving our neighbors."

Two hours later, while I'm taking a short afternoon nap, the phone rings. It's Mr. Mario.

"We're neighbors," he says, "but we've never been in each other's homes."

That's true. He lives only a few blocks away.

"How are you feeling?" I ask him.

"Low."

"Well, you've only been home for a couple of days. You have that nurse coming over?"

"She comes over but I don't need her. You used to come visit me at the hospital, but now that I'm home I see the visits have stopped."

"Mr. Mario," I say, "if you're inviting me over, why don't you just say so?"

"Shakespeare expressed it best through Falstaff in *The Merry Wives of Windsor*. Falstaff was talking about a woman with whom he was flirting. He said that 'she gives the leer of invitation.' "

"I'm not sure I understand," I say. "Who's doing the leering— you or me?"

"Pastor," he says, "I see you as an innocent of heart. If there's any leering going on around here, it's coming from me."

"It sounds like you're lonely, Mario, and could use a good home-cooked meal."

"Music to my ears."

"Well, you've cooked me enough meals over the years. I'm glad to reciprocate. How about a healthy vegetable stir-fry?"

"More music. I'm practically out of bed and doing the booga-loo."

"I'll be over at six. I'll provide the ingredients, you provide the pots."

"Deal."

It has been over a month since the death of Mario's wife but I could feel her strong presence in their cute little house on Arling-ton Avenue. When it comes to the interior of a home, you can feel a woman's touch. The windows are accented with bold print curtains that give an arty modern flavor. In fact, the entire house is arty—interesting wooden furniture, bookcases with dozens of literary works including, of course, many different editions of the complete works of William Shakespeare. Above the fireplace is a big portrait of Shakespeare framed in bronze. I get the idea that Mario worships Shakespeare.

"I do," he tells me when I comment on the portrait.

Mario is looking amazingly healthy for a man who has been through his recent ordeals. He's sitting at the kitchen table watching me cook.

"Shakespeare," he continues, "was not only the greatest poet who has ever lived but the greatest dramatist and observer of the human condition. His psychological insights into people are astounding. But he didn't just look into their minds and behaviors, Albertina; he looked into their souls. He saw all our essential conflicts and expressed them in language that soars with beauty and grace."

"Did he find answers to those conflicts?" I wonder.

"He saw that the answer is to bring the conflicts to light, to allow them to live and, as the poet John Keats put it, haunt our days and chill our dreaming nights."

"Did he believe in God?" I ask while cutting up the carrots.

" 'There are more things in heaven and earth,' Hamlet told Horatio, 'than are dreamt of in your philosophy.' "

"Meaning?"

"Meaning, Albertina, that Shakespeare understood that the mysteries of the supernatural are vast. He held to no traditional religion. His intellect wouldn't allow it."

"Does that mean that great intellects have always rejected great religions?"

"That's a trick question, Albertina. You know the answer is no. Saint Augustine was a great intellect and so was Thomas Aquinas."

"Both believers."

"Yes, both believers. But the works of Augustine or Aquinas have not edified and delighted millions as have Shakespeare's."

"They were thinkers," I say. "Shakespeare was an entertainer. Unfair to compare them, isn't it?"

"Hard to discuss this with a woman who's looking for logic."

After dinner, our discussion continues. I'm fascinated by Mario's mind. I love it when he quotes the old poetry and even acts out whole scenes from Shakespeare. He plays all the characters and has all the lines memorized. He acts with bold gestures and great flair. Time flies by and, before I know it, it's ten o'clock.

"Way past my bedtime," I say.

"And I haven't even told you my plans to reform the culinary habits of our people."

"Glad to see you ate well tonight, Mr. Mario."

"Miss Albertina, I had no idea you had such a command of healthy cooking."

"My mother and grandmother both knew their vegetables," I say. "It wasn't all pork and fat in our house."

"Then I can recruit you in my campaign to keep our people from eating themselves to early deaths?"

"Only if I can recruit you into my campaign of showing all people how the Jesus I love defeated death?"

"So it's a standoff between me and you, is that it, Albertina?"

"No, Mario, it's a friendship."

The Waldorf

"**D**on't sound like no friendship to me," says Justine who's driving me to the airport. On a fine May day, I'm off to Nina's bridal shower in New York. "Having lost one wife, sounds like Mr. Mario is looking for another."

"Justine," I say, "the world to you is nothing but wall-to-wall romance. You don't see it any other way."

"Not trying to see it no other way. Why should I? Without romance, we might as well be dead. And right now, for a righteous preacher, you're far from dead. You're in the thick of two hot romances."

"Child, what in the world are you talking about?" I ask.

"I'm talking about a disc jockey who's five years older than you and Mr. Mario who's five years younger. Girl, you're sitting pretty."

"I don't believe either one of them has that kind of interest in me."

"Want me to call them and ask?"

"No, I don't."

"See there, you're scared of the truth, Albertina."

The truth is that I'm carrying two gifts, one from Mario and one from Clifford, but I am not about to tell Justine. That'll only convince her that her romance theory is right. I prefer to see the gifts as tokens of friendship.

Thirty minutes later, as the plane levels off after a smooth takeoff, I open my tote bag and bring out the presents. Clifford's is a CD of Ella Fitzgerald called *Like Someone in Love*. I slip it into my Discman and listen to the first song, "There's a Lull in My Life." I wonder about the meaning. Then I open Mario's gift, a lovely bound edition of Shakespeare's sonnets. I see that Mario has earmarked Sonnet 17 and the lines.

If I could write the beauty of your eyes,
And in fresh numbers number all your graces,
The age to come would say, "This poet lies,
Such heavenly touches ne'er touch'd earthly faces."

With Ella singing sweetly in my ear and Shakespeare filling my eyes with beautiful imagery, I feel light-years younger. I feel like praying.

"Father God, thank You for music and thank You for language. Thank You for letting us turn sound to beauty and words to poetry. It is Your grace that offers us unending love, even those of us who cannot sing like Ella or write like Shakespeare. Thank You for setting our minds at ease, for allowing us to create great flying machines that navigate the skies like birds. Thank You for the friends we make and the trips we take, the adventure of this life that You have so wonderfully given us. Living this life with You inside my heart is the greatest gift of all. You are with me, Lord—on this plane, in this song, in this sonnet. I love this gift of life and pray that I live it as an expression of gratitude. In Jesus' name, Amen."

I ride with Ella, Shakespeare, and the Lord all the way across the country, sometimes drifting off to sleep but always awakening with a smile. Another song, another sonnet, another moment of comfort and appreciation for the healing miracle of art. I stop to eat a cheese sandwich—they don't give you much on planes these days—and a little later I plug in the headset to see what music the airline has programmed. When I switch on the jazz channel,

I'm delighted to hear all my old friends: David Fathead Newman, Johnny Coles, Marcus Belgrave, Hank Crawford, each a master of his instrument. After the last song, Hank Crawford playing "Misty," a soothing voice shocks me out of my reverie. "This is jazz deejay Clifford Bloom for American Airlines, hoping that my choice of jazz gems was to your taste and wishing you a most pleasant voyage. Now let's hear from Miles Davis. . . ."

I can't help but smile. Clifford's tastes and mine are identical.

The song says "April in Paris," but I'll take May in New York. I thank God for traveling mercies and getting me here safely. It's springtime and the city is decked out in its finest. The leaves are budding in Central Park. Flowers are blooming in little boxes set out in front of the Waldorf Astoria Hotel. The city folks are actually friendly. I check in, have a bellman carry up my luggage, and find myself in a pretty pink room facing Park Avenue. There's a message from my son, Andre, saying he'll be here by eight to take me to dinner, which means I have time for a little nap. When I wake up, I remember my dream was about Arthur. It's no surprise since it was at the Waldorf where I first met Arthur, my second husband and my daughter Laura's daddy.

Forty-something years ago, I'd been called to New York City by my friend from Memphis, Bobby Blue Bland, the great blues singer. He needed a support vocalist for a big tour he was doing with B.B. King, starting out at the Fillmore East. I was in between gigs and happy to accept. Just to hear Bobby sing every night was a great joy. He sang like Reverend C. L. Franklin preached. The man's a master.

The Waldorf was filled with party people. I loved the blues music, but I never loved the blues life. Because Bobby was putting me up at a fancy place like the Waldorf, I thought the scene would be calmer than it was back on the chitlin circuit. It wasn't. Mind you, this was the late sixties. This was the day of "anything goes." My room was next to a big suite where some of Bobby's people were carrying on like crazy. The noise was getting to me. I didn't want to scold them and bring them down, but neither did I want to listen to the commotion. So I went downstairs to sit in the lobby and read a book. It wasn't the Bible but something related to religion: a collection of writings by James Baldwin, talking about how he grew up as a boy preacher in a storefront church in Harlem. I love James Baldwin.

"My, my, that's some serious reading," said a man walking by me on his way to the bar. He was wearing a Bobby Blue Bland satin baseball jacket.

"I'm Albertina Merci," I said. "I'm singing with Bobby. Are you with the band?"

"No, I'm the road manager. My name's Arthur Brand. Everyone calls me A."

"Nice to meet you, Mr. Brand," I replied, not looking to get too familiar. At the same time, I couldn't help but like him immediately. He had soft brown eyes, beautiful dark skin, and a radiant smile. Plus, his voice was soothing. I'm a fool for men with soothing voices.

"I think I saw you when you were singing with Ray Charles. Didn't you once sing with RC?"

"Oh yes," I said, smiling at the memory. "I worked for Mr. C."

"Well, Miss Merci, you look a little lonely sitting here. If you'd like to join me in the bar for a drink, I'd be honored."

"Don't take offense, but I'm comfortable right where I am."

"Then may I get myself a little taste and come join you right here?"

"Please do."

"And there's nothing I can bring you?"

"A ginger ale would be nice."

"One ginger ale coming up."

Hard as I tried, I felt myself attracted to this man—even in those very few minutes. Arthur had a way about him. You could feel his soul when he talked to you. He was genuine.

That feeling was confirmed when he came back with ginger ale and sat across from me. Turned out his room was on the other side of the party suite and the noise had bothered him too.

"Life on the road is mighty rough," he said.

For the next two hours, we talked like we'd known each other forever. He laughed easily and made me laugh. He'd grown up in Louisiana and knew all the greats like Guitar Slim and Percy Mayfield. He knew everyone in the business, but he wasn't a name-dropper. I could tell he was a worker. He had never married and had no children. I was divorced. He wanted to know about my first husband. The question triggered a twinge of pain. He could see it on my face.

"Don't need to talk about it," he said.

Yet, strangely, I wanted to. And I did. I told Arthur, a perfect stranger, how my first husband, Dexter, had been a womanizer.

"And you didn't know that from the start?" he asked.

"No," I said. "Had to learn it the hard way."

"Well, that's how I learned about women."

"And what is it that you learned?"

"The same, I suppose, that you learned about men," he said. "They're not to be trusted."

"I didn't say that."

"No, but I can feel that in you. I don't blame you for that feeling. May even be a good thing. You need to protect yourself. You're too nice a woman to be hurt again. Well, I better turn in. Long day tomorrow. Look forward to working with you, Miss Merci. Good night."

And with that, he excused himself. In spite of having three drinks in the course of our conversation, he never got rowdy or rude. Never made an advance. He was a perfect gentleman.

During the two-month tour we became friends. At first I was standoffish. After Dexter, I had built up a wall and kept all men out. I didn't trust them. I didn't want to get involved and risk getting hurt again. Yet I did get emotionally involved with A, I did fall in love, I did marry the man and have my daughter, Laura. I did see that all my instincts about him were right: he was a good and gentle soul. But I also saw that, for all his goodness, his heavy drinking was more than a way to relax; it was a serious addiction. Our life together was sweet but short. Liver cancer took him when Laura, our first and only child, was still an infant.

Arthur taught me to trust again. He taught me to love again. But thinking back on how we first met here in the Waldorf, I remember how that love ended practically just when it started. I think of the song that says, "There's a Lull in My Life."

Dinner with Andre

My son is talking about his father, and the topic doesn't make me happy. He knows that. Andre is a considerate young man, but in this instance he has no choice. He's telling me about his wedding in June and preparing me for the fact that his dad and his dad's wife will be attending.

"Of course he should attend," I say. "He's your father and he loves you."

The truth is that my former husband Ben Hunter *is*, in spite of everything, a loving father. He is devoted to Andre, just as he was devoted to Darryl. He suffered over Darryl's death just as deeply as I did. After Ben and I divorced, after he married the woman he had been carrying on with while he was still married to me, he kept up with his boys. It turned out she was a successful businesswoman who owned a beauty shop and, from what I heard, had a knack for snatching other women's men.

But all that's in the past. The present is filled with promise. My son is doing well at his craft. He's forging a successful career in the highly competitive world of screenwriting. Sitting across from him in a little Italian restaurant in midtown Manhattan, I look at his face and remember how, as a little boy, he loved to read adventure books and invent stories. I can't help but be proud that he has turned that passion into a profession.

"I'll be glad to see your father," I say. "I know he's your biggest booster, Andre, and I'm grateful for that."

"Mama, you know I'm grateful to God for both my parents. I'm grateful that things are finally going my way. I can't tell you how glad I am to be out of that marketing job and writing full-time. And glad to have finally found my soulmate in Nina."

I nod my head. Inside my heart, though, I worry about my son. I love him dearly. As a little boy, he was the sweetest thing ever. He still is. He's a trusting soul, but when it comes to women he has always been naïve—at least in this mother's opinion. Maybe I'm being too protective of my son, but time and again I've seen how a beautiful lady will take advantage of him. I definitely put Nina in that category.

"Nina," he says, "is really happy you're coming to the shower, Mama. It means a lot to her."

"Wouldn't miss it for the world, son."

"Tell me about Mr. Mario," he asks. "You said he's making a strong recovery. Have you seen him lately?"

"Saw him the other day, baby," I say. I explain Mr. Mario's latest passion for healthy foods.

"You need to put him in touch with Walker Jones," Andre insists. "He's on the same kick. In fact, he has hired Nina to be the model in his exercise video. She's with him tonight at a studio going over the plan."

My heart sinks. I know Walker Jones. He had an affair with my neighbor Justine and dropped her like a bad habit. Then while he was having an affair with talk show host Maggie Clay, Maggie caught him with another woman. By coincidence, Nina and I were in Dallas last year at the same time. So was Walker. That's when I saw him going into Nina's hotel room at night.

But what can I say? Nothing. Months ago I told Andre that I

had doubts about Nina. As I see it, a word to the wise is sufficient. But it breaks my heart that, in this area of his life, my son seems to lack wisdom. My only alternative is to pray that I'm wrong about all this.

The shower is not a happy event for me.

I'm glad that Nina enjoys being the center of attention. After all, that's the point of a shower. But she seems to be overplaying the part of the happy bride-to-be. Her enthusiasm feels contrived to me. Her friends are other actresses and models, all of whom appear twenty pounds underweight. Nina pays little attention to me. Her focus is on the gifts. I feel isolated and irrelevant. As I move around the party, I overhear several of the guests whispering less-than-flattering things about Nina. They talk about her fickleness and her obsession with her career. Why should the atmosphere be so catty? Aren't these her closest friends?

I smile through the first two hours. Then I feel the need to excuse myself.

When I say good-bye and kiss her on the cheek, Nina couldn't be sweeter. She turns to everyone in the room and says, "I hope you all have met Andre's mom. She's a pastor and she's an absolute doll. Thanks for coming, Alberta."

In order to avoid embarrassing Nina, I don't correct her by saying that my name is Albertina, not Alberta.

Satellite Fellowship of Faith

Back from the wedding shower in New York, I hit the ground running. I speak to our neighborhood grocers about donating food for our twice-weekly dinners for the homeless. The response is good. I also go to the hospital to visit two parishioners, an elderly woman who has suffered a stroke and a young man who has miraculously survived a car wreck. I pray with both these believers, thanking God for the opportunity to minister to them.

Now I'm in my office in the House of Trust, going over plans for next month's auction/dinner that will support half a dozen scholarships for bright inner-city children in need of financial help.

Denise, a church member who donates her time to help me with administrative duties, calls me on the intercom.

"Bishop Henry Gold is calling from his car," she says, "and wants to know if this is a convenient time to stop by and see you."

"Bishop Gold from Dallas?"

"Yes," says Denise. "The one who's on TV all the time."

Strange, I think to myself. *Why would he want to just stop by like we're old friends?* I've met the man a couple of times, but we've never said more than a few words to each other.

"Tell him I'm happy to see him, Denise," I say, curious about what this could be about.

I met Bishop through Maggie Clay, the talk show star. When my niece Cindy died of cancer, Maggie designated Gold to officiate at her memorial service. My children and Cindy's friend were peeved that I didn't officiate—Cindy was like a daughter to me—but I decided that a funeral was no time to raise a ruckus. I've heard Bishop preach several different times. He's a great performer but, to be honest, I've never been moved.

I look out my window and see a stretch limo pull up to the church. A driver runs out and opens the door. The Bishop emerges, followed by a younger man who looks just like him.

"Pastor Merci," says Bishop as he steps into my office, "a pleasure to see you. May I present my son, Reverend Solomon Gold."

"Nice to see you, Bishop. Pleasure to meet you, Reverend. Would you gentlemen like some coffee or tea?"

"Oh, we're fine, Pastor," says Bishop, who has a full head of silver hair, dark brown eyes, medium-brown skin, and what appears to be a small fortune in jewelry adorning both wrists. Solomon has less gold but exudes the same aura of well-being. The men are dressed in immaculately tailored suits, white shirts, and elegant ties. Their black shoes shine like mirrors.

"Don't want to take up your valuable time, Pastor," says Bishop, "so I'll get right to the point. I'm here because Los Angeles is the second target in our Satellite Fellowship of Faith expansion program."

"Pardon me, Bishop," I say, "but I thought your church was called the City of Faith."

"It was, Pastor, but when we initiated our expansion plan it became obvious that no single city could contain us. Therefore we rechristened ourselves Fellowship of Faith."

"I understand."

"I'm happy to report that we have bought up the land on this long block of Adams Boulevard where we plan to build our first Fellowship of Faith in southern California. The majority of merchants are thrilled because we are paying considerably over market price. Your church, which I understand was a generous gift from our mutual friend Maggie Clay, sits right in the middle of the block. Since your gain from the sale of the building and land will be pure profit, I know you'll be delighted with our offer. You'll be able to build a much bigger church with bigger facilities. God does indeed work in wondrous ways."

I'm floored. My first reaction is *No, you just can't come in here and buy up our church.* But I don't say anything—not yet.

"Solomon will be leading this Satellite Fellowship of Faith," says Bishop.

"Our real estate division back in Dallas has partnered with the best real estate agents in Los Angeles," Solomon says. "We'll do all we can to help you relocate and find land at the right price. We will not abandon you, Pastor. We aren't that kind of people."

What kind of people are you, I want to ask, *who come in here and simply presume I'll let this church be torn down without a single objection?*

"We've brought the papers," Solomon continues, reaching in his attaché case, "that explain the terms of sale. If you'd care to sign them today . . ."

"Gentlemen, gentlemen," I say, "I must stop you here. No papers will be signed today. I do not lord over a congregation. I serve a congregation. I answer to a board of trustees."

"I don't have to remind you, Pastor Merci," Bishop quips, "that most congregations trust their ministers implicitly. If the minister is clear in her intention, the congregation will follow."

"At this moment," I say, "this minister is anything but clear."

"This is not a confusing matter," the Bishop insists. "It is, in fact, a wonderful opportunity for your church and mine. Not to mention what it will do for this troubled neighborhood. Our mammoth facility will include not only a gorgeous sanctuary, but a recreation center, a school, and a Starbucks."

"I could use a latte right now," I say. The men smile, but only slightly. They're all business.

"This decision will take some time," I add.

"Can we have your initial reaction to our proposal?" asks Bishop.

"The thought of tearing down something we've worked so hard to build up is not immediately attractive," I say.

"You don't want to think of yourself, Pastor," says Bishop. "You want to do the will of God."

"I'm not thinking of myself, Bishop, I'm thinking of my congregation. I'm also thinking that God's will is something we must discern for ourselves. I'd love to tell you how God's will is manifesting in your life, Bishop, but I'm afraid I have no idea."

Bishop Gold does respond. He offers me a small smile, a weak handshake, and a quick, "Solomon will be in touch with you, Pastor."

The clergymen reach for their cell phones and leave. Within seconds, the stretch limo, with curious neighborhood kids chasing after it, is heading down Adams Boulevard.

God, I pray, *I give You praise and I give You glory. I pray to do Thy will, whatever that will may be. I thank You for Your presence, God, and I thank You for Your guidance. Amen.*

Lake Hollywood Reservoir

"God is nothing but a figment of your imagination," says Mr. Mario as we walk around the water reservoir nestled in the Hollywood Hills. The circular path covers a little over three miles. Oak trees and wildflowers surround us. It's a delightful place to exercise.

"God," I say, "*is* our imagination. God is our everything."

"It comes down to this," says Mario, who three months after his heart attack is moving slowly but steadily. "You think God created man. I think man created God."

"I want to concentrate on nature," I say, "not theology."

"Your nature is far too sweet, Albertina, and your approach far too nonconfrontational. Someday I will provoke you into a verbal battle to the death."

"I doubt it," I say, laughing.

I'm feeling good. I'm wearing a brand-new Adidas workout suit that Laura sent me from Chicago. It's a little too racy for me—the bold purple-and-white stripes are designed for teenagers, not old ladies—but the fabric is light and my jogging shoes are so cushiony I feel like I'm walking on air.

I'm just happy that Mario has recovered and gotten back into the swing of things so quickly. He's wearing a gray sweatshirt and baggy black sweatpants. His white baseball cap says OREGON SHAKESPEARE FESTIVAL. Since his heart attack, he's lost weight. He's still heavy, but nothing like before.

"If I get to walking too fast," he says to me, "just say so."

"I'm doing fine, Mario. I can feel you're in a hurry, but you've always been in a hurry, haven't you?"

"Not like now," he replies. "In the past, I was moving fast, but moving in the wrong direction. Now I'm headed right, Albertina, but I have no time to waste. Fact is, I feel downright guilty for all the time I've wasted and the damage I've caused."

"Guilt is a heavy burden," I say. "I wonder if it's necessary."

"I agree that guilt can be crippling," Mario says. "Claudius, Hamlet's uncle, declares, 'My stronger guilt defeats my strong intent.' But I do not intend to let guilt slow me down or knock me off course. If guilt does nothing but motivate me, I welcome guilt."

"You welcome pain, Mario? You welcome shame?" I ask.

"I recognize that such emotions are inevitable. We can't remove them. The trick is how we use them."

I'm about to say that God can remove shame because God has forgiven us, even if we can't forgive ourselves. But I decide, at least for now, not to waste my breath. Mario will only argue and this setting is too lovely for an argument.

But Mario is a talker, and Mario is on a mission, and people on missions tend to be nonstop talkers. He's talking about the books he's reading on diet, exercise, health, and the sicknesses suffered by African Americans.

"I'm taking off another two months to do nothing but study and read," he says. "I'd like you to join me in this effort."

I'm a bit taken aback. Part of me wants to tell Mario about Bishop Gold's visit to my church—how deeply that upset me. But Mario is hardly the man with whom to discuss church matters. Besides, he has his own agenda.

"I want to be frank with you, Albertina," he says. "I want to let you know that I want a companion on this long journey."

The statement has me worrying that the concern I've shown for Mario since his heart attack together with the loss of his wife has given him the wrong impression.

"We are all companions on the journey of life," I say. "We're all here to help and love one another. That's the divine commandment of the man I call Jesus."

"When you bring Jesus into the conversation," Mario quickly replies, "you push me out. Is that your intention?"

"Not in the least."

"And, as a pastor, don't you have to be concerned with your parishioners' physical health?"

"Yes, but, above all, their spiritual health."

"There you go—you're back to Jesus."

"I'm *always* back to Jesus, Mario. That's never going to change."

"You're too smart a woman to be taken in by that hocus-pocus. Your mind is too keen to be distracted by fairy tales. One day you'll stop talking that silly language of superstition."

"God *is* my mind. He *is* my language."

"Shakespeare said, 'Women speak two languages—one of which is verbal.' "

"It's the language of the heart that we need to heed. That's what I believe, Mario."

"And what is the language of your heart telling you now, Albertina?"

"It's not my heart, it's my legs. They're practically screaming. After all this walking, it's time to stop."

Whole Foods

Justine and I are at the checkout stand at Whole Foods supermarket. She has loaded her shopping cart with fried chicken, macaroni and cheese, and a small mountain of potato salad, not to mention a large apple pie.

"The point of shopping here," I tell her, "is to stock up on nutritious foods."

"That rabbit food you're buying doesn't cut it, Albertina. Besides, the prices are crazy. If I'm going to overpay, I might as well buy stuff I like."

"Sweetheart," I say, "I thought you were on the Palm Beach plan."

"My doctor says that diet is dangerous."

"And didn't he give you another one?"

"I'm testing out different ones," Justine says. "We'll call this the Whole Foods diet."

Driving back home in my PT Cruiser, we stop at the corner of Washington Boulevard and LaBrea Avenue at the U.S. Post Office that's named for Ray Charles. I won't buy my stamps anywhere else. While I'm in line, I notice Justine talking to the branch manager, a good-looking man in his forties.

Afterward I ask Justine, "Wasn't that man you were talking to once our mail carrier?"

"Sure, that's Clarence, Clarence Withers. We were renewing

our friendship. He has moved up in the world. I was joking with him. I said, 'Brother Clarence, just 'cause you're running this office doesn't mean you don't deliver anymore, does it?' 'Sister Justine,' he said, 'you can still count on me for home deliveries anytime.' He's coming over tonight for apple pie. And he's bringing the ice cream."

"What about your friend Johnny Marbee from Target?"

"Johnny is visiting his mama in Virginia. Besides, our arrangement is not exclusive. It's more a matter of convenience."

I start to say something, but better sense gets hold of me. Justine does not take well to my preaching. She and I have had this talk before. If I even subtly suggest that she's overindulging herself with men and food she'll accuse me of being a puritan, so I leave it alone.

I arrive home and discover a message from Reverend Solomon Gold, Bishop's son. He wants to have another meeting. I'm a little taken aback that he called me at home, not at church. I think that's presumptuous. In any case, I don't want to deal with it now. Instead the spirit tells me to call Mario.

He picks up on the first ring.

"Hope I'm not disturbing you," I say.

"Never, Albertina. You aren't the disturbing kind."

"I think I have a ministry for you, Mario."

He laughs. "Long as it has nothing to do with that church of yours," he says, "I'm willing to listen."

"You've never even been to that church of mine," I state.

"Nor do I intend to."

"This would involve going to church only to discuss a non-church issue."

I explain that I would like him to talk to our members about healthy food.

"I'm not ready," he says.

"Not ready to step foot in a church, or not ready to talk about food?"

"Both. And even when I am ready to talk about food, it won't be in a church. I don't want to give the impression that I endorse the sloppy sentiments of any Christian church, even yours, dear Albertina."

"My, my, my," I say. "You do have an attitude."

"I call it having integrity."

Later that evening, while I'm watching the nightly news on PBS, the phone rings. It's Clifford Bloom. He's perky beyond his usual level of high energy. He's positively joyful.

"Albertina," he says, "you've been on my mind all day. All day I've been sitting here listening to King Curtis."

"Aretha's sax player?"

"The same. He's wonderful."

"Lord, have mercy, Clifford, if there's a bigger soul music fan than you I don't know who it could be. Don't know anyone else who can listen to King Curtis for eight straight hours."

"You don't like him?" he asks.

"Love him! Knew him even before he signed up with Atlantic and went on the road with Aretha."

"So you know 'Memphis Soul Stew.' "

"Yes, indeed," I say, "with all that fatback bass."

"Well, they're having a Memphis Soul Revue concert at Shrine Auditorium. Curtis, of course, is long gone, so is Otis Redding and Rufus Thomas, but Carla Thomas will be there, and so will Sam Moore, Booker T. Jones, and Isaac Hayes. What do you say?"

"I say you sound excited, Clifford."

"We could have dinner, or not—whatever makes you comfortable, Albertina. But this is the music you love. It's the music I love, and it'd be great if we could love it together."

Is he being too forward or just plain nice?
After all, Clifford *is* the nicest of men.
"What do you say?" he asks.
"To be honest, I'd love to see my old friends."
"And I'd love to make new ones."

The Abundance of Things

I read the Bible every night before going to sleep. My mother taught me that, not by instruction but by example. Example is always the best teacher. Mama would sit in a rocking chair by the side of her bed and read for a good half hour. She moved her lips as she read, and often when she came upon an especially moving verse, she closed her eyes. When her devotional time was over, she pressed the Bible to her breast and said, "Thank you, Lord, for speaking to my heart."

Tonight the gospel of Luke is speaking to my heart. In the twelfth chapter of Luke, a man comes to the Lord and expresses fear of losing an inheritance. Jesus says, "Take care to protect yourself against every desire for having more, for life does not lie in the abundance of things one owns."

I love the phrase "abundance of things." I think of how when I was younger a love of "things," as opposed to God's love, pushed me off track. Back then you couldn't have told me I had gone astray. After all, I've always believed in God.

I was out there on the road. I was singing solo gigs, I was doing background work, I was running in and out of the studios in Los Angeles, Chicago, and New York. I was doing pretty well. Getting along and going along at a pretty good pace. Then the script got flipped. Soul music was in decline. Disco was hot; deejays were hot; live music was not. Soul singers didn't matter the way they used to. I was suddenly knocked back on my heels.

That's when I met Ben Hunter.

When I met Ben, I was living in a one-bedroom apartment in Inglewood, not far from the Los Angeles International Airport. It was just me and Laura.

Ben, the leading salesman in all of California for Allstate Insurance, had sold me a policy. Because Arthur had died penniless I wanted to protect my daughter should anything happen to me. I was taken by Ben's easygoing demeanor. Of course it didn't hurt that Ben knew who I was and liked my singing. He was a vigorous man with a quick smile and warm manner. He slightly resembled Count Basie's singer Joe Williams, and I confess to having had a secret crush on Joe for many years. Ben spoke with great confidence and came with high recommendations from two friends. I bought the insurance policy and, a week later, accepted his invitation to dinner.

The courtship was intense. Ben was in a hurry. He had been a widower for over a year and was eager to remarry. His first wife had died in a horrific car accident and he suffered mightily from guilt. The day it happened he asked her to pick up his dry cleaning. On her way a drunk driver ran a red light at eighty miles an hour, blindsiding her. She was pregnant. Ben couldn't stop asking himself, "Why not me?"

He saw in me and Laura an instant family. I saw in him a good man and a good provider. He had a lovely home in Baldwin Hills. He drove a Mercedes. He owned a condo in Las Vegas. He had an abundance of things. On the spiritual side, he belonged to a big church on Crenshaw Boulevard and tithed regularly. He pursued me relentlessly.

Grief is a strange phenomenon. It hangs around like the plague, eating at you, corroding your soul. I had been grieving for Arthur. Ben had been grieving for his wife. Grief brought us together, and, I suppose, grief was transformed into romance. Or maybe grief was simply suppressed. I really don't know. All I do know is that, despite some misgivings, I accepted Ben's proposal. He respected my insistence that we not be intimate until after our marriage. That endeared me to him even more.

The wedding was larger than I wanted, but Ben had literally hundreds of good customers and good friends. We honeymooned at a posh hotel in Hawaii. He satisfied me in all ways. Two months later, I was thrilled to learn that I was pregnant. Andre was an easy baby. Darryl came along only thirteen months later. Darryl was a difficult infant, but Ben was a wonderful hands-on father. Life was good.

Funny how good can turn bad in the blink of an eye. Ben's business began to falter. It wasn't due to drink or drugs. Because Arthur had been an alcoholic, I had vowed never to go near a man who had self-destructive habits. But I didn't know that the need to acquire things could be the most self-destructive habit of all. I was interested in security and Ben seemed to offer me security. I saw security in his possessions—our homes, our cars, our comfortable lifestyle. The relentless improvement of that lifestyle, though, became Ben's obsession. He bought a third home up at Lake Arrowhead; he bought a fancier Mercedes; he bought himself handmade suits and a diamond pinkie ring larger and far flashier than the wedding ring he had given me. I didn't mind. He worked hard for his money, and if he wanted to reward himself, fine. I didn't need jewelry. Security was enough for me. But when Ben's financial world began to crumble, I saw my security crumbling as well.

Ben was overly ambitious. He was also overextended. Unknown to me, he had bought a printing plant in Whittier and a storage warehouse in East L.A. He didn't know much about either business, but saw them as guaranteed moneymakers. In frighteningly quick succession, both businesses failed. A third enterprise, an ATM franchise, was even more disastrous. These ventures not only drained us of our savings but put us deeply in debt. He lied to family and friends about our condition. Because his entrepreneurial adventures had been so distracting, his core income—insurance sales—had suffered enormously. Allstate threatened to fire him. He didn't know where to turn. Because I was out of the loop—I let Ben take care of our finances—the negative news came to me only in dribs and drabs. I was too busy enjoying the abundance of things to see the light. I was too busy living in a world of false security. When that world fell apart, I woke up.

Finally I realized that not only had my husband put himself and his family in an impossible financial situation, but that he was steadfastly refusing to admit it. Pride kept him from admitting failure. Pride kept him from altering our lifestyle. The condo in Vegas and the place in Lake Arrowhead were gone, but when I suggested we sell the house in Baldwin Hills and move to a more modest home, he flatly refused. He refused to sell his fancy car; he refused to let the world know that our prosperity had vanished.

Only later would I learn that he'd turned to LaVern Green, a woman who owned the most successful beauty salon in South Central L.A. Ms. Green was also a licensed real estate agent who sold homes to the stars. She was wealthy and lived in a house twice the size of ours in Baldwin Hills, ironically only three blocks away from us. Also ironically, she attended the same church we did. I saw her merely as a woman who liked flashy clothes and attracted many men—but the irony caught up with me when the rumors reached my door. I ignored them at first. I didn't want to believe them. I didn't want to believe that Ben was living a double life. For all his problems, he was still a devoted dad. He wouldn't do this to me. I knew unfaithful men—my first husband, Dexter, had been unfaithful—and Ben was not unfaithful. No one could tell me he was.

But I knew. Women always know. Sometimes—often, in fact—we won't admit it, even to ourselves. But something deep inside us, a feeling in our gut, isn't right. Something gnaws at us.

That something grows. Suspicions mount. Trust is undermined by undeniable evidence: the way he won't look you in the eye; the way your intimate times are fewer and fewer; his disinterest in what you are wearing and what you are saying. And then comes the day when he drops the bomb.

He still can't look at you. His eyes are darting in every direction. He can barely get the words out.

"I'm leaving," he finally says. He doesn't give a reason.

You force the issue. You ask him directly, "Is there another woman?"

He won't answer.

And on that horrible day when my trust in the abundance of things came crashing down, I forced the answer. "Is there another woman?" I repeated.

When he still refused to say, I knew it was the truth. No response was the surest response of all.

My husband was leaving me for another woman.

In his mind, this other woman would save his life, save his image, salvage his self-worth, give him all the cash and social status he needed. Not only was he moving out; he was moving on and moving up. He never shirked his duties as a dad—I'll forever give him credit for that—but I was history. Ben found someone who could provide him with an abundance of things.

That was a lifetime ago. It took me another lifetime to learn to offer the pain of that experience up to God. God could handle it. But back before I started to walk with the Lord, I couldn't. I couldn't see how I could live with the hurt and humiliation. There's a Teddy Pendergrass song that says, "The Whole Town's Laughing at Me." That's the song I played over and over again back then. That's the song I couldn't get out of my head.

Finally I had to ask God, "Why? What's wrong with me that I keep picking the wrong man? What's wrong with my judgment? How can I be so naïve? How can I be so stupid?"

Change of Plans

It's the second week in June. I'm all packed and ready to fly to Andre's wedding in New York. My plane leaves at two p.m. That same day, at ten a.m., Solomon Gold is scheduled to meet me in my office.

At ten on the dot, my nephew Patrick sticks his head in the door.

"Can we talk?" he asks.

"I have a meeting, Patrick."

"I know," he says. "It has been canceled."

"First I'm hearing about it."

"Solomon called me."

"You know him?"

"I went to theology seminar with him."

"He didn't mention that when I met him," I say.

"You didn't mention your meeting with him and his dad to me either," says Patrick.

"I was going to," I assured him. "Just been busy."

"Anyway, Solomon and I had dinner last night and he explained the situation."

"I see. And how do you assess it?"

"Interesting."

"Interesting good or interesting bad?"

"Interesting good. I see it as an opportunity for us to expand our church."

"Our church seems to be expanding at a pretty steady pace the way things are right now."

"This is a big bump up, Aunt Albertina. We'll get an incredible cash influx and be able to build a church twice the size of this building on a parcel of land with room for future expansion."

"If expansion is the goal," I say.

"Expansion is inherent to Christianity. The idea is to spread the Word. We're evangelists, aren't we?"

"We are indeed, but it's always a matter of how to expand, and when."

"This seems obvious."

"Well, I see you have a strong opinion, Patrick, but what about the rest of the congregation? We serve them."

"We lead them."

"We need to hear them," I remind him. "They come first."

"I agree," he says, "but Bishop and Solomon are serious about this location. We're their only obstacle. There are hundreds of locations they could choose in L.A. I'd hate for them to change their minds."

"Is that what Solomon says—that they may change their minds in a hurry?"

"He has insinuated as much."

"And he sent you to bring the word to me."

"I think Solomon is sincere. And I respect the way his dad turned Fellowship of Faith into a national phenomenon. Bishop Gold has become a superstar in the Christian world."

"I thought the Christian world had only one superstar. And his name is . . ."

"His name is Jesus," says Patrick, "and you're right, Aunt Albertina. I just meant that I respect his uncanny ability to work the media."

"Is that a Christian virtue?" I ask.

"It is if you're spreading the Word. Anyway, I'll tell them we need time."

"Please do."

"How much time, Aunt Albertina?"

"We'll schedule a meeting with all our church members when we get back from the wedding. Until then, I'll be praying about it."

I arrive at the New York Hilton a day ahead of Patrick and the rest of the family. I want time to get over my jet lag and be in the Word. When everyone gets here, especially Andre's dad and his wife LaVern, I want to be prayed up. I want to be deep into forgiveness, gratitude, and love. I have no intention of ruining my son's wedding. My prayer is to be a simple instrument of love.

That evening I go downstairs and have dinner at Green Life, a pleasant health-food restaurant, and feel my instrument breaking down when I see Walker Jones, the exercise guru, sitting at the next table. He's with a famous African American actress whose name I can't remember. He spots me before I can look away. He smiles, waves, and comes over.

"Pastor," he says, "what a great pleasure to see you. I knew you were coming in for Nina's wedding, but I'm delighted you got here early. If you're dining alone, I'd be honored if you would join us."

"Thank you, Mr. Jones," I say, "but I'm just having a quick bite and going back up to the room. I'm a little tired from the trip."

"I can understand that, Pastor. Please let me know if there's anything I can do to make your stay here more comfortable. After all, with Nina as the spokeswoman for my new video series, we're practically family."

I force a smile. Everything I say to Walker Jones is forced.

God forgive me, but I don't like the man. Don't trust him. His words are hollow and his style is slick. I know how he played my friend Justine; I know how he played TV star Maggie Clay; I fear that he's playing Nina. But I don't know. I don't want to know.

My dinner is ruined, my appetite gone. I take a couple of sips of soup and a small bite of the vegetable plate. I ask the waiter to give me a doggie bag. Maybe I'll eat later in my room. For now, I'm out of here. But before I scurry away, Walker catches my eye and blows me a kiss from across the restaurant. I'm feeling sick inside.

Back at my room, I'm feeling poorly. My stomach is in revolt. Maybe it was something I ate on the plane. Maybe it's nerves, but all of a sudden I'm weak and feverish. I can't hold down my food. I'm regurgitating, even when there's nothing left inside my belly. The pain is intense. I get dizzy and fall down in the bathroom trying to make it back to the bedroom. This is bad. I'm never sick. Haven't had a cold in years. Never get the flu. I exercise regularly and eat moderately. Now the thought of any food sickens me. It takes a lot for me to even consider calling a doctor. If I were home, I might. But I don't know any doctors in New York and don't want to disturb Andre on the night before his rehearsal dinner and two nights before his wedding. Besides, his friends have taken him to a bachelor party. So I'll ride it out. I'll just stay in bed and breathe, drink lots of water, get lots of sleep. But I'm too weak to lift the glass of water and sleep won't come. The stomach pain is too sharp to let me doze off. The stomach pain goes from bad to worse to excruciating. I start imagining what could be wrong. I start moving into fear. I know I have to turn off my imagination. I know I have to turn to God. I pray my condition will pass.

When daylight breaks the pain is still present.

What to do?

I can't miss the rehearsal dinner tonight at seven p.m. and I have to feel better before the wedding tomorrow because I'm officiating. I can't miss the Sunday morning brunch because I'm hosting, along with Laura.

At nine in the morning Laura calls from the airport. She has just arrived from Chicago. She hears I'm not right. I don't go into details. I understate my condition. "By the time you get here, baby," I say, "I'll be fine."

When she gets here, I am not fine. I am suffering even more.

"I'm calling a physician," my daughter states with absolute assurance. "I don't trust hotel doctors. Andre will give me a reference."

I ask that she wait another few hours. She refuses. Through Andre she finds a doctor, makes an appointment for two p.m., and by one-thirty has managed to get me downstairs and into a cab.

Laura is holding my hand. A team of specialists, called in by Andre's doctor, has put me through a battery of high-tech exams and scans. My pain is so severe I can barely listen to the physicians, but I catch the words "gallbladder disease" and "gallstones" and "laparoscopic surgery." My gallbladder is infected and needs to be removed immediately. I don't want to do it. I'll miss the wedding.

"You'll miss more than the wedding if we don't act on this now," says one of the doctors.

I want to ask more questions, but the pain has taken over. I'm given a shot and now I'm drifting off, drifting off, finally free of pain. . . .

The Great Physician

We make plans and expect them to work out perfectly. A wedding is the ultimate plan. In the case of my son, Andre, his fiancée Nina even hired a wedding planner. Everything was thought out, every detail scrutinized and systematized. I had observed all this from a comfortable distance in L.A. All I had to do was show up, officiate at the ceremony, and cohost the day-after brunch. But even the brunch, down to the color of the napkins, was orchestrated by the wedding planner. All I had to do was offer up my credit card.

I was happy with the arrangement. This was my debut as a mother-in-law and I adamantly did not want to be interfering or controlling. I did not want my reservations about Nina to influence my behavior. I tried to do what was asked of me as lovingly as possible.

But God looks at our fastidious plans and smiles. He sees us trying to control every facet of our lives and our future. He understands the human need to do that, but eventually we must understand that His plans, not ours, prevail. That's tough because His plans are often unforeseeable and indiscernible. We know His love, we feel His goodness, but we can't always see the big picture. That picture changes from day to day. So all we can do is go with the flow.

This Tuesday morning I'm looking for that flow. I'm looking for the rhythm of my recovery, and I haven't found it. These past days haven't been easy for me; they haven't been easy for anyone.

I'm on the eighth floor of a hospital in New York City. My room is a little cramped. Outside my window I hear the roar of traffic. Cabs are honking like crazy. My head is pounding like crazy. Laura is helping me get dressed. Laura has been by my side since the operation.

Three days have passed since my gallbladder was removed. The surgery went well. Laparoscopic surgery, with its small incisions and minimal invasion, is a miracle. The infected gallbladder and the inflamed gallstones are gone. No tumors, no cancer. I'm achy but thankful that the prognosis is so good.

Meanwhile, the wedding plans have had to be radically altered. Instead of the ceremony being held Saturday night, it's being held today in the hospital chapel. The party and dinner went on as scheduled without me, but Laura convinced Andre to convince Nina that the ceremony itself would have to be pared down to accommodate only immediate family and the closest friends. She also convinced Andre that I should still officiate. The doctors assured her that I could be wheeled downstairs to conduct a short ceremony.

At the same time I'm happy and unhappy. My pain and my gratitude are both great. I cannot thank the Great Physician enough for saving my life. He saves it every day. I owe Him everything. He is blessing me with the opportunity of doing something I have long desired to do. I'm performing my son's wedding ceremony.

But my vanity is wounded as it has never been wounded before. My vanity is crying out. I realize that this is my flesh, not my spirit, but at times like this the flesh is strong. I had picked out my dress at Saks Fifth Avenue in Beverly Hills only a few months ago. Justine had gone shopping with me for three long days until we found the right outfit. The black dress, with silver stitching and small brocade design, was quiet and tasteful and absolutely elegant. It flowed just right. The dress subtly elongated my figure and made my good posture look even better. All this is pride, I realize, but it's my son's wedding and I wanted to look my best; I wanted to put the best face on my youthful appearance. I confess that, in front of Ben Hunter and his wife, LaVern, I wanted to look absolutely smashing.

In truth, I look absolutely pathetic. Seated in a wheelchair, I feel like an old lady. The black dress looks crumpled and creased. I need to stand to show its smooth line, but I can't. My hair has been through hell in the operating room and can't be styled the way I had planned. Laura had to find me a wig. The wig's a little too big and the curls a little too curly. I feel foolish. There's no time to get another one. As Laura and I ride down the elevator on the way to the chapel, I have no choice; I must give up my pride to God, leave my ego at the door, and accept that His plans, not mine, are the only plans that matter.

It doesn't help that everyone is seated in the chapel waiting for me. It doesn't help that LaVern looks like she's had a face-lift. Her skin is tight, her bodice revealing, and her neck covered in pear-shaped diamonds and glittering gold. I have to admit that she looks younger than when I saw her last. Ben looks older, but he is dressed in a fabulous custom-made silk suit. On his right wrist is a gaudy diamond Rolex. On the temples of his oversized glasses I see the double Gs that stand for Gucci.

Nina got her looks from her mom, whose name is Sylvia. Like Nina, she was a model before becoming an actress. She works in dinner theater companies all across the country. Nina's father is nowhere to be found. Andre told me that he disappeared when Nina was three.

LaVern is loudly glamorous; Sylvia is quietly glamorous; I am not glamorous at all. Oh, how I want to be! There are times when glamour is called for, and a wedding is one of those times. Sitting before these two glamorous women, I'm feeling like an invalid. The truth is, at least for now, I am an invalid.

Accept God's plan, I pray to myself. *Lean on Him.*

My wheelchair is wheeled to the altar. I am facing the congregation. Recorded music is played over loudspeakers. Nina has chosen Luther Vandross singing "Here and Now." That's fine. I love Luther. The sound of his voice comforts and calms. When I see Ben escorting Andre down the aisle, my heart swells with gladness. My vanity dissolves. My son is beautiful. It no longer bothers me that he looks like his dad. His dad is beautiful. Ben and I conceived a beautiful human being. And suddenly I am overwhelmed with gratitude that, despite my emergency operation, my son has agreed that I should be at the altar doing the honors.

Thank you, Jesus.

Thank you, Andre.

As Nina's mother walks her daughter down the aisle, I see two stunning women and find inspiration in their beauty. I praise God for his ability to create beauty in so many forms. Physical beauty can inspire us to seek spiritual beauty.

"Spiritual beauty," I say in my opening remarks, "is the beauty I'm feeling in this chapel today. That's the beauty of Jesus Christ. It's His presence I'm feeling. I'm feeling Him. We don't know what He looks like, so we can't worship the way He looks. Fact is, every culture gives Him a different look. Every painter gives Him a different face. But it isn't about looks. It's about spirit. It's about the thing we can't touch, the thing we can't see, but the thing— the beautiful, everlasting holy thing—that we can feel. Yes, I'm feeling Him in this chapel. I'm feeling Him when I look into the eyes of my son, when I look into the eyes of his beautiful bride, Nina, when I look into the eyes of Nina's beautiful mother, Sylvia. I'm seeing Jesus in the eyes of Andre's beautiful dad, Benjamin, and his beautiful wife, LaVern, in the eyes of my beautiful daughter, Laura, and my beautiful nephew, Patrick. I'm seeing Jesus wherever I look. He is here. He is among us. He is blessing us with grace. He is blessing this couple with a love that lasts far more than a lifetime, but forever and a day."

As I speak, I realize that the real miracle of Christ is His ability to change lives. Changing water to wine is one thing, but changing human hearts is another. For all the animosities in that chapel—for all the animosities in my own heart—He prevails. He washes over the bad feelings with His forgiveness. He brings Himself into the center of the ceremony through the words I speak.

I say, "Jesus, we are here to honor You because You change us into forces of goodness and light. Your truth is that the celebration of marriage and the celebration of love and the celebration of Christ are all one. Our marriage to You is the true commitment. We mirror that commitment in this ceremony today. We are committed to the constancy of love. It never stops. It never falters. It never fails to refresh and renew. As Andre and Nina commit to each other, we recommit to You. Your story of rebirth is the story we continue to follow. It's the story that gives shape and sense to our lives. It's the story we're telling today. It's the story, Almighty God, that we will tell as long as we have breath to speak and a voice to sing.

"Somebody give God a praise! Somebody give Him Glory! Say, 'Glory! Glory! Glory to the Living God! Glory to the Living God!' "

The little chapel starts rocking with praise. I hadn't planned this, hadn't even foreseen this, but somehow the Holy Ghost comes down and the place catches fire. There are only a handful of people in the chapel, but folks are standing and calling His name. Arms are waving. There's dancing in the aisles. Folks screaming, "Hallelujah! Hallelujah!" We're praising Him, we're lifting Him up, and I'm so glad about it. So glad that my son is being married, right here, right now, where Jesus is the joy that gets us to moving and shouting, and God's great spirit is coming down like thunder and lightning, and everyone is glad, everyone is jumping, everyone is acting like we're not in a hospital in New York City, but having church in Mississippi. It don't matter, though. Don't matter what we looked like when we came in here, don't matter what we had been thinking or feeling because God has changed all that. God has made this a holy place where holy matrimony is a Holy Ghost celebration of His glory and His Grace.

Praise Him! Just go on and Praise Him.

The Rock That Will Not Move

The older I get, the closer I get to God. I love it. I love this process of aging, not because I want to look wrinkled and haggard—I want to stay young and look good as much as anyone—but because the more I live, the more I see His reality as the only reality. When the kids say, "Keep it real," I think of God. He's as real as you get. The further you get from God, the less real you are.

All this is to say that my sickness was a blessing. It connected me even more closely to the source of my well-being. It also made me appreciate more keenly the glorious gift of life.

When I got home from New York, Laura took time out from her teaching job in Chicago to stay with me till I got back on my feet. I told her that it wasn't necessary. Justine and other friends would look after me. But Laura wouldn't take no for an answer. She wasn't going to let her mama be alone. So she stayed for a week, waiting on me hand and foot. Each day she helped me do my walking. At first it was slow going, but little by little I was able to pick up the pace. My doctor in L.A. claimed he'd never seen such a strong recovery from that particular operation.

My nephew Patrick preached in my place until I was well enough to get back to church. When I did return, the congregation couldn't have been sweeter. Everyone expressed concern. It was wonderful to see how much they cared, but after Laura left I had almost too many caretakers. Justine wouldn't leave me alone, treating me like I had a month to live. Clifford Bloom brought over dinner along with the newest gospel CDs by LaShun Pace and Helen Baylor, two of my favorite singers. When Clifford wasn't there, Mr. Mario was. He took over my kitchen on two occasions, preparing fresh fruit salads and three kinds of brown rice.

"I've been reading up on the gallbladder," he says, "and I think you need to consult a dietitian, Albertina. I'm studying with a brilliant man at UCLA. Will you come along with me next time I see him?"

"I agree about the relationship between diet and gallbladder disease. I've been studying the issue myself. I've posted a strict eating plan on the door of my refrigerator. You can see it for yourself—lots of fluids and high-fiber foods. Low-fat dairy products. No red meat. No fried foods. No salad dressing other than olive oil and vinegar. Believe me, Mario, I'm taking this seriously."

"I still think it would be a good idea to see my man at UCLA."

"I'm so behind on my ministerial duties," I say, "I have to concentrate on church."

"It makes me sad to hear you talk that way."

"Why? It makes me happy, Mario."

"It's an illusion. Your religion is a fantasy."

"Please, let's not get started on that again," I say.

"Last night I was reading about Einstein, a man of no small intellect," Mario continues, "and I came upon this quote from him. He put it plainly: 'I do not believe in a personal God . . . If something is in me which can be called religious then it is the unbounded admiration for the structure of the world so far as our science can reveal it. . . . I cannot conceive of a God who rewards and punishes his creatures, or has a will of the type of which we are conscious in ourselves. An individual who should survive his physical death is also beyond my comprehension; such notions are for the fears or absurd egoism of feeble souls.' "

"So you're accusing me of having a feeble soul, is that it, Mr. Mario?"

"I think you have a noble soul, Albertina. But your cultural influences have blinded you."

I pause before responding. I pray before responding.

"You know, Mario," I finally say, "no one I know has fallen in or out of love with God because of an intellectual argument."

For the moment, Mario stops to pause and reflect on what I've said.

Score one for Jesus.

I take the Fourth of July holiday to build up my strength. It seems that while I've been recuperating, Bishop Gold and his son Solomon have been contacting individual members of House of Trust and spelling out their arguments for why we should sell. Several of those parishioners have called me to ask where I stand. I tell them that later in the month we'll have a meeting to voice our views.

I'm furious at Bishop for going behind my back. I try not to think about it at the big picnic Justine is having in her backyard. She has tons of food—pork, pies, slabs of ribs, vats of potato salad—and good ole soul music blasting from speakers placed on the patio. She and Clarence Withers, her friend from the Ray Charles Post Office, are grinding to Millie Jackson's suggestive grooves. Millie is crazy.

I leave early. Still can't stop thinking about Bishop and Solomon campaigning among my membership.

I call Patrick.

"Have you heard what your friend has been doing?"

"Solomon?" he asks.

"Solomon and his daddy both."

"They've been expressing their opinions," says Patrick.

"Before we've had a chance to express ours to our members. You think that's right? You think that's respecting our leadership position in our church?"

"I told you they were in a hurry, Aunt Albertina."

"And I told you, Patrick, this is nothing we can deal with hastily."

"Well, you were sick, and that took some time."

"And it will take some time before these gentlemen will get an answer. Do you want to make that clear to them, or should I?"

"I have made it clear."

"But they keep on sneaking behind our backs."

"They don't see it as sneaking. They see it as doing us a favor."

"We don't need any favors, Patrick. God favors us with all we need."

"This is the real world, Aunt Albertina."

"Amen," I say, "and I've been living right in the middle of it as long as I've been alive."

An hour later, the phone rings again.

I pick it up.

"Albertina," says Justine in a voice that's barely audible. "You gotta get over here. You gotta call an ambulance."

Signs

Sickness can be a sign. It can be used to teach. Before our very eyes, Mario became suddenly sick. Then his wife died of sickness. My own disease descended upon me without warning. And now Justine has been struck. Her condition is critical. All this is running through my mind as I sit in the ambulance with her on the way to Cedars-Sinai. These sicknesses, these signs, one after another. What is God saying? What am I to do?

I pray, not to beg God, but to reconnect with Him.

Teach me, I pray, *to read You right*.

Justine's relatives arrive after we do. I tell them she's suffered a heart attack and the cardiologist is with her now. That's all I know. A little later, Johnny Marbee arrives, Justine's friend and Target coworker. His physical stature and outgoing personality remind me of Justine.

"She talks about you all the time, Pastor," says Johnny. "You're such an important part of her life, you have no idea. Just yesterday she was saying how she never makes a move without your advice."

"Justine is a beautiful person," I say.

The doctor arrives. Elliott Henderson is a middle-aged black man with a gentle manner. He's thin and oval-faced with small rimless glasses that give him a professorial air. "Her arteries are badly clogged," he says. "But she's stabilized and it looks like she's going to get through this thing. That heart of hers is strong. But we need to go in and clean out the arteries."

"An angioplasty?" asks Johnny.

"Yes, exactly," says the physician.

The relatives gather around me and ask me if I'll pray with them.

We hold hands and hold up Justine in prayer for several minutes.

Afterward an elderly aunt asks me if I know Justine's age.

"Forty-nine," I say.

"So young to be so sick," says the aunt.

It's the middle of the night when Justine regains consciousness and recognizes me sitting next to her. She looks like she's been to hell and back.

"Your prayers got me through," she says.

"Baby," I say, "God got you through."

"God is good," she whispers.

"All the time," I confirm.

I'm in Justine's hospital room the next afternoon when Dr. Henderson gives his prognosis.

"Your condition is the result of your lifestyle," he tells Justine. "Bad nutritional habits. Lack of exercise. A lifetime of ingesting the wrong food."

Justine is weak but still strong enough to protest. "Doc," she says, "I'm never gonna look like Britney. I ain't ever gonna be skinny."

"I'm not talking about skinny," the physician is quick to reply. "Shapes are shapes. Sisters have unique bone structures and body types. There's nothing wrong with being proud of your unique frame. There's nothing unhealthy or unflattering about being big and strong. Embracing that physical reality is great. Being obese, though, is fraught with life-threatening dangers."

"I'm hooked on junk food," Justine admits.

"The whole country's hooked on junk food," the doctor says. "It's an addiction."

"How do I break the addiction, Doc? Give me the diet. Give me the plan. I've tried 'em all. All of 'em work for a hot minute, and then I'm back where I started."

"I understand," Dr. Henderson says. "There are a million methods out there, and none of them are foolproof. It's not a question of magic; it's a matter of knowledge, discipline, diet, and exercise."

"I'm a disciplined worker, Doctor," says Justine. "But when it comes to men and food, my discipline never seems to kick in."

"Before you leave the hospital, I'll have some suggestions for you."

Even in her weakened condition, Justine is straining to see if Dr. Henderson is wearing a wedding ring. He isn't.

"Suggestions about food or men?" she asks slyly.

The good doctor smiles and answers with a single word, "Lifestyle. It's all about adopting a healthy lifestyle."

The Last Supper

Back in the spring, before going to Nina's wedding shower at the Waldorf, I had my first interfaith meeting with members of Rabbi Naomi's congregation and parishioners from House of Trust. We met at Temple Abraham where the rabbi and I led the discussion. Because Passover and Easter were only a week apart, we discussed the meaning of the Seder, the ceremonial meal that has been an annual event for Jews ever since the exodus. This same celebration brought Jesus to Jerusalem nearly every year that He walked the earth. Leonardo da Vinci's famous *Last Supper* is a painting of Jesus at the Lord's last Seder.

Naomi explained the significance of the Seder for the Jewish people. She said it was a sacred obligation, a scriptural mandate. She quoted from Exodus 13:3: "Moses said to the people, 'Remember this day in which you went out from Egypt, from the house of slavery; for by a powerful hand the Lord brought you out from this place.' " The theme of the holiday is freedom, the rabbi explained. The holiday lets us all relive the exodus by highlighting the source of all true freedom, God. As Rabbi Cohen spoke, her biblical images came alive, her stories flowed with excitement. My parishioners focused on her every word.

I, in turn, explained the significance of the Seder for Christians. In the gospels of Mark and Luke, we read how Jesus sent His disciples into Jerusalem to celebrate Passover in an "upper room." I mention the beautiful Mahalia Jackson gospel song "In the Upper Room," where she imagines herself "talking to my Lord." I even sing a couple of bars of the song. I show how Jesus' Last Supper was a pivotal point between his entry into Jerusalem and his Crucifixion. It was at the Seder that Jesus gives bread to his disciples, saying, "Take it; this is My body," before asking them to drink from his cup. "This is My blood of the covenant, which is poured out for many." The Seder is where we are introduced to the mystical moment in which we can absorb Jesus.

At the Seder, Jesus knew He was going to die; He knew He would rise again; and He foresaw that Peter would deny Him three times.

"For both Christian and Jew," I said, "the Seder is an ongoing source of rich symbolism and soaring inspiration. I love the holiday with all my heart."

Afterward there were questions from both Naomi's group and mine. We had a lively and good-hearted exchange. No one got angry. No one started preaching. And no one hurled accusations. Naomi's people were curious about Christianity, and mine were curious about Judaism.

"We're deeply connected," I said before the colloquy ended. "We're connected by history, by blood, and by the loving God we all serve."

My nephew Patrick declined to participate. He had broken off his relationship with Naomi and thought his presence would make her uncomfortable. Afterward, when he asked me how it went, I said, "Beautifully."

"What about the divinity of Christ?" he asked.

"What about it? He is surely divine."

"Did you get Naomi to admit that?"

"That didn't come up."

76

"So you skirted the issue."

"No, that wasn't the issue."

"How could it not be?" Patrick asked. "That's the essential tenet of Christianity. That's the basic issue. Either Christ is God or He's not."

"I didn't go there to debate, Patrick, I went to listen and to share my faith in God."

"How can you do that without discussing Jesus?"

"I did discuss Jesus. Jesus was the focus of my remarks."

"Then you confronted Naomi and her parishioners about their denial of His divinity."

"I did no such thing. I spoke of our Lord with reverence and love. It's possible to do that, you know, without confronting anyone."

"It sounds to me like you compromised, Aunt Albertina."

"Patrick," I said, "when have you ever known me to compromise my belief in Jesus?"

"Never."

"Then why would I start now?"

"Naomi," he said.

"Why would Naomi cause me to compromise?" I asked.

"You don't want to alienate her because you're somehow convinced our relationship can be salvaged."

"Baby," I told my nephew, "that is straight-up ridiculous. I'm no matchmaker and I don't believe in romantic interference. If I don't do it with my own children, I'm sure not doing it with my nephew."

"I guess I'm uncomfortable that you and Naomi have developed a relationship."

"I can understand that," I said, "but you've chosen not to be involved, and I respect that choice."

"So she was comfortable in addressing our people?" he asked.

"Extremely," I answered. "In fact, Patrick, she *is* our people."

That was back in April. It's now late July. Justine is due home from the hospital tomorrow and I'm almost completely recovered from my operation. Patrick has been one of my most attentive caretakers during this trying period, and I love him dearly. But Patrick, bless his heart, is still obsessed with Naomi. Even though they haven't spoken in months, he can't stop thinking about her. Take tonight.

He and I are going to the big concert hall on South Vermont Avenue where the Crenshaw Christian Center is presenting Fred Hammond. I look at Fred as the gospel Stevie Wonder. He can write, sing, and harmonize with absolute brilliance and anointing. The concert is thrilling and the presence of the Living God strong. Patrick is as moved as I am, and driving me home, he asks me whether I think Naomi would have liked the music.

"She would have loved it," I say. "I've seen her CD collection. It's filled with gospel."

"Well, how can she love the music and reject the message?"

"Maybe she doesn't reject the message. Maybe she just sees the message differently than you do."

"There's only one way to God. And that way is through Jesus."

"If Jesus is about understanding and compassion and we believe in following His example, maybe it's a good idea to understand people and show compassion for those who see the message differently."

"That depends on the difference," says Patrick. "I want to know the ways in which she perceives the message differently."

"Then ask her," I urge.

"You're telling me to see her again?"

"You sound like you want to see her."

"Maybe that's the enemy pushing me on."

"Or maybe it's your heart."

"I'm too proud to beg."

"Beg for what?"

"Reconciliation."

"We always want to reconcile our differences, don't we? Listen, Patrick, you're getting too worked up. Just take my place when Naomi and her group come to the House of Trust for the second of our interfaith meetings."

"Just like that?" he asks.

"Just like that," I answer.

Community in Conflict

As usual, time's flying by. But this year time's flying at the speed of light. So much has happened: In February, Mario had his heart attack. In March I was watching Nina trying on gowns at Saks. In April I was at her shower in New York. In May, Mr. Mario was back on track, walking me around the reservoir. But come June my health fell apart at Andre's wedding. A month later, it was Justine's turn. Now it's August and I can't put off this meeting about selling out to the Fellowship of Faith. The meeting is long overdue.

I've decided to let everyone have their say, including Bishop and his son, who have flown in from Dallas for the occasion. I want everyone to hear everyone else's position out in the open. I want to stop the secret campaigning and bring everything out into the open.

It's Tuesday night. Earlier today it was nearly ninety degrees. The temperature has dipped, but it's still warm. Parishioners are cooling themselves with fans donated by the neighborhood mortuary, which, by the way, is being bought up by Gold.

The church is packed to capacity. Patrick, Bishop, Solomon, and I sit in chairs facing the congregation, one hundred strong in addition to merchants whose establishments will be affected by our decision.

I start with prayer. "Let us do Your will, Father God, and find the enlightenment to understand that will."

I want to be fair, so I allow Bishop and Solomon to begin. They open a large briefcase that contains a computer and, within seconds, initiate a PowerPoint presentation on a pull-down screen. Up pops a professional full-color rendering of this first Satellite Fellowship of Faith. The complex is enormous, the sanctuary a dramatic dome, the school building a four-story structure, plus parking garage, gym, and a minimall for Starbucks, Jamba Juice, and a Christian multimedia entertainment store. As the presentation unfolds, I hear gasps from several of my church members. Gasps of excitement, I presume, not gasps of horror.

In addition to showing us why it will be good for the neighborhood to build this new Fellowship of Faith, I feel Gold luring my members to his church. When he describes the sixty-member choir he plans to recruit and the ten-piece band who will accompany them, when he shows pictures of the giant revolving screens that will flank the dais and the ultra-plush oversized velvet seats in contrasting shades of blue and green, there's no doubt he's seducing my people. And then, when he culminates this irresistible sales pitch by describing the financial windfall that our House of Trust will enjoy, I wonder how in the world should I respond.

Before I do, though, I ask two of our prominent members to express their opinions.

"I've lived in this neighborhood my whole life," says Sister Hortense Singer, "and I want my church in this neighborhood. It was a blessing when Pastor Merci moved in here, and I want that blessing to continue. I see no reason to change."

"The reason to change," says Brother Brad Woodson, "is to improve. Why not get a bigger church with more land? Besides, there's lots of land in this very neighborhood."

I ask Phillip Ash, president of our congregation, what he thinks.

"Pastor," he says, "we want to know what *you* think. You secured this building. You began this church. Through Christ, you led us here. We're dying to know your opinion, Pastor."

"Thank you, Phillip. I'll tell you plainly. At my age, moving is no easy thing. In some ways I feel like we just got here. The offer is certainly generous, and it is tempting, but I'd like a great deal more time to think about it. If we do move, what land around here really is available? And if we rebuild, how big do we build? How do we feel about 'bigness'? I like to think of House of Trust as a congregation that cherishes intimacy, intimacy with each other and intimacy with God. Do we lose that intimacy if we start on an ambitious move-on-out and move-on-up program? Will our energy be expended on expansion rather than on the Lord? Do we want the bureaucratic headaches that come with a church that borrows from the corporate culture?"

"What about our associate pastor?" asks Brother Brad. "What's his view?"

"I've known Solomon Gold since seminary," Patrick says, "and consider him and his father men of God. Like Pastor said, it's early in our deliberations, but I favor progress and growth. To me, progress and growth don't have to exclude God; those forces, in fact, can glorify Him even further."

There's more discussion before I suggest a nonbinding preliminary vote, just to get a sense of how the congregation feels. The vote is remarkably even. Someone counts and comes up with a dead tie. And that's excluding our merchant neighbors, who have refrained from voting.

"I suppose we need to form a committee," I suggest, "to gather more information. If we do sell, where do we buy, how do we build, and what are the costs? The committee will also meet individually with congregants to gain a fuller sense of their points of view. I'd like to head this committee and ask Patrick, Sister Hortense Singer, Brother Brad Woodson, and Brother Phillip Ash to serve along with me."

"We'll need an answer by the end of summer," says Bishop.

"Fine," I say, "by the end of October you'll have an answer."

"I was thinking of the end of September," Bishop retorts.

"The end of October," I say calmly, "gives us all time enough."

"If we find another location for the Satellite Fellowship of Faith before then—" Bishop starts to say.

"Then that will solve the problem," I finish the sentence for him.

Walker's Wonder Program
of Mental and Physical Health

Walker's program of weight reduction and exercise hasn't changed since I started seeing his infomercials last year. The only difference is that Walker has hired a model/actress to demonstrate his exercises and to pitch his products. She is my daughter-in-law, Nina. Their infomercial seems to be on television night and day. You can't escape it. From my point of view, they're selling sex, not health. They're selling perfectly molded bodies and the fantasy that one day your body can be just as sculpted.

I have to hand it to Walker. He fooled Justine last year when he used her to get to me so I, in turn, could get him to TV superstar Maggie Clay. He played both Justine and Maggie; while having affairs with them, he was carrying on with other women as well. He played everyone, and even when he was caught, he found a way to bounce back and stay in the spotlight. That brother is slick. He's attractive and smooth talking and brimming with ambition.

When Andre called me after he and Nina had returned from their honeymoon in Bermuda, I didn't bring up the infomercial. But he did. This was back in July.

"Have you seen Nina doing those TV ads?" he asked.

"I have."

Silence.

"Well," he said, egging me on. "What did you think?"

"Now, baby," I said, "why would you ask me what I think when you know what I think."

"You don't approve."

"It's not for me to approve or disapprove, sweetheart. It's not my business."

"You know, Mom, it has been absolutely great for Nina's business. Three different producers have seen those infomercials and offered her roles."

"Good," I said.

"Good roles. Serious roles. Nothing frivolous."

"I'm glad, honey."

"Are you really?"

"Andre, why are you asking me these questions? If you're comfortable with all this, that's all that matters."

Silence.

"Well," he finally said, " 'comfortable' wouldn't be the right word."

"Then what is the right word, baby?"

"Maybe 'uneasy.' "

I sighed to myself. I prayed for the right words, the right approach. There was another long and awkward silence between us.

"You want to talk about it, sweetheart?" I asked.

"Not now, Mom."

"No problem. I understand. Whenever you feel like talking, I'm here."

"I'll be feeling better when her work with Walker Jones is over," he admitted. "There's something about that guy. . . ."

I said nothing.

"I love you, baby," I told him.

"Love you too, Mom. I'll call you next week."

A month has passed since Andre and Nina's honeymoon and since Justine's angioplasty. Justine seems to be doing okay. Dr. Henderson is pleased with her progress. He says she is an extremely determined woman. He doesn't know the half of it. Justine keeps insisting that he pay her a house call. He keeps saying that would be unprofessional. "Maybe it would be unprofessional," Justine says, "but it sure would be fun."

Now Justine is asking me, "Have you seen that fool Walker Jones on TV with Andre's wife?"

"I was just on my way over to your place, honey. I'm bringing you some soup I made last night."

"I'm all souped out, Tina," says Justine. "If I don't see another bowl of soup for the rest of my life that'll be soon enough. You don't need to come over. I'm okay. Now about those commercials. What does your son say?"

"What can he say?"

"He can tell that wife of his to keep away from that jive turkey—that's what he can say. Have you warned him?"

"In so many words, yes."

"Well, I don't need so many words. I just need one word—trouble. That girl's trouble. Andre's in trouble. Their young marriage is in trouble."

"I see your spirit is back, Justine."

"The devil attacked my heart, not my head. My head's clear as a bell. Andre is cruising for a bruising, and it's your job to head him off at the pass."

"I don't see it that way."

"Then how do you see it?"

"God is writing the story of our lives, not you or me."

"You mean to say that we can't change the story if we want to?"

"We can mess up the story if we think we're in charge," I say.

"We can get willful and controlling. But if we give Him the control and seek to follow His will, He will live out His story through us. We will be His instrument. Others will see His victory in our story."

"And you really believe that, Albertina?"

"With all my heart."

Can I Get a Witness?

Clifford Bloom is the most patient of men. As a faithful member of House of Trust, he knows what I'm going through.

"Anytime you want to talk about it," he says, "call me. I'm a good listener, Albertina."

"I know you are, Clifford, and I appreciate it."

He asks me out on numerous occasions, but invariably I refuse. The more I refuse, the more understanding and patient he becomes. He seems never to take my refusals personally. He never fails to say, "No hurry. No problem. We'll get together whenever the time is right for you. Take as much time as you need."

To be honest, I find his patience a little trying. But who am I to be impatient with someone's patience? That's kind of crazy, isn't it? On the plus side, because Clifford is a jazz deejay and a convert to Christianity, we always have much to discuss. He genuinely loves the Lord. The fact that he has a sonorous radio-friendly voice and looks sixty-five, not seventy-five, adds to his appeal. And no woman minds a man who is attentive to her every need.

I finally accept an invitation to lunch at the Ritz-Carlton Hotel in Marina del Rey. Our table is on the outdoor patio facing the marina. The September day is glorious, the boats gleam in the afternoon sun. We're sitting across from *Grand Destiny*, a fabulous yacht fit for a king. In the distance, someone is playing an acoustic guitar. I recognize the melody as "The Shadow of Your Smile." I think of Marvin Gaye's version of the song. Marvin sang it magnificently.

"On a little-known record issued after his death," says Clifford, "Marvin Gaye sang 'The Shadow of Your Smile.' He overdubbed it so that his falsetto shadowed his natural voice. Leave it to Marvin to use a recording technique to mirror the song's title."

"I love the way he did it," I say.

"So you know it, Albertina."

"Every last riff of it."

"So we're thinking the same way," Clifford concludes.

I have to agree, but I'm uncomfortable saying so. What does it mean that this man is reading my mind? Am I resisting something that shouldn't be resisted?

It's time to order. I'm in the mood for a niçoise salad, but I let Clifford order first. I'm just curious about what he will say.

"I'll have the niçoise salad, please," he tells the waiter.

"The same for me," I say.

Clifford smiles. His smile says we are in tune. But are we?

"You must be tired from preaching this morning," he says.

"I hope my sermon didn't tire you out."

"Never, Albertina. Your sermons energize me. I only asked about your being tired because I'm going to a revival meeting tonight with some folks from the music industry, and when I mentioned I went to your church, they asked if you might come and give your testimony."

"Which folks?" I ask.

Clifford mentions several singers, producers, instrumentalists, and arrangers. I knew every last one of them. I've worked with most of them.

"I didn't know they were interested in the Lord," I say.

"I didn't either," explains Clifford, "until I started mentioning my own faith. You know how faith is contagious."

"What time?"

"I could pick you up at about eight."

"That'll make three times you've been with this old minister in one day, Clifford. I hate to put you through that."

"It's a blessing."

Come eight o'clock I'm ready. I'm actually eager. Clifford drives us over to a stately house in Hancock Park where everyone he mentioned is waiting for us. Old home week. Most of the music people are black, but there are a few white executives who signed me to deals back in the day. These are Jewish friends of Clifford's. Clifford seems to be having an impact on a whole mess of folks. Clifford is sure-enough serious about Christ.

We sit in a big living room. It's all very comfortable—easy chairs and couches, tea and coffee and little cakes. Clifford introduces me in very simple terms. "You knew her as a singer," he says. "I know her as a pastor. In both capacities, she's wonderful—Pastor Albertina Merci."

"I'm not giving any sermon," I say. "I'm just talking among friends tonight. So good to see old friends. So good to hear your voices and know you're curious about my story. Gonna sound corny, but I can't help it—with so many of you, we made beautiful music together. So thank you.

"Well, I'm keeping this story short. I'm giving you the edited-down version. I'm saying that I'm living in His grace, and the reason for that is that I accepted Him as Lord and Savior. I always loved Him. Loved Him as a child and Loved Him as a teen. Loved Him because Mama passed on His love to me. Saw Him in her and liked what I saw. But then the world turned. The world pulled me in.

"I was singing in nightclubs when I was too young. Went on the road when I didn't even know what the road meant. Worked in studios when studios were wilder than the nightclubs. Y'all know what I'm talking about."

Everyone breaks out laughing.

"Yes, indeed. Married young. Married wrong. Vowed to get marriage right so I got out. And thought I had it right when I married Arthur. Many of y'all knew him. Beautiful man. Supported my singing career. Did all he could for me. But he didn't do enough for himself and drank himself to an early grave. May God have mercy on his beautiful soul. Some of y'all knew my third husband, Ben. That didn't work too well either. When he left, it took me a little time to put myself back together, but I did it. Revived my career, started recording again, and found someone to book me.

"That brings me to a cold winter night in Jackson, Mississippi. I'm in a motel room, all by my lonesome, on a chitlin-circuit tour with Johnnie Taylor and Betty Wright. These words come to me. Don't ask why. Don't ask how. They just come.

"I start singing. . . .

Moon is howling outside my window
Wind is crying and I'm staring at the phone
Mama said, "There'll be nights like this, child,
When a man loves you, then leaves you all alone."

Got the sanctified blues . . .
I miss the church where Mama raised me

Got those sanctified blues . . .
Miss the wisdom that Mama gave me

Sanctified blues . . .
This man ain't what he said

Sanctified blues . . .
Said he was a saint, then led me to his bed

When that church got to shoutin'
And the Holy Ghost ran up and down the pews
I saw this man with pretty brown eyes
Saying, "Girl, let me spread the good news."

Sanctified blues . . .
Oh, he looked so fine, his words were strong and true

Sanctified blues . . .
Lord, have mercy, if only I knew

"I work up a quick arrangement with the band, and for the rest of the tour I'm singing that song. Folks go crazy. Can't get enough of it. I know I have me a hit. Big hit.

"But then one night in Lexington, Kentucky, I heard the Lord's voice saying, 'Albertina, go home.' I think I'm hearing things, so I ignore the voice. But then it comes back. And back. 'Go home.' God keeps talking as clear as day. But what does that mean? Takes me a while to see it means go home to God.

"So I go. Go back to school and get a divinity degree. I love the courses even though a lot of the male teachers don't look kindly on female pastors. That didn't bother me because I was there to learn, not to get their approval. Before I got saved, I needed everyone's approval. Once I got saved, I got the only approval I ever needed—God's, an unconditional approval based on His grace. Then I learned the Bible in Hebrew and Greek so I had the righteous reference for helping people properly.

"When I got out, I didn't have a church or a congregation, but, thanks to my 'Sanctified Blues' royalties, I did have a house and enough money to raise my kids. Best of all, the old me was dead, and the new me, the one born again in Christ, was alive and kicking. I no longer worried about who would accept me, or whether my style of singing was in or out of fashion, or whether I'd wind up a bigger star than Gladys Knight or Chaka Khan. The biggest star of all told me I'd live forever. When you believe that, folks, all that other ego stuff loses its power.

"So this life I'm living is Christ living through me. That's the change. It's *His* story, not mine. I've turned my life over to Him. I'm talking to y'all tonight not because I have to, not because I've been told to, but because it *feels* good. Don't you know that God feels good? God feels better than anything else in this mean old world."

When my testimony is through, Clifford is overjoyed. His eyes are dancing. He can't stop thanking me for attending.

On the ride home he says, "Albertina, I knew you'd reach these people, but you did it in a way that really penetrated their hearts. That's why we love you so much. That's why I . . ."

He stops midsentence, and I'm grateful.

Sessions of Sweet Thought

"I say keep God out of the equation," Mario announces with his typical bravado.

"I can't," I admit.

We're taking a brisk walk around the track at the Jim Gilliam Park high atop LaBrea Avenue. Seems like Mr. Mario and I have become exercise buddies. It's early morning and the sky is a little smoggy, but nothing like it will be later in the day. The downtown skyscrapers loom in the distance. A news helicopter hovers overhead. Mario and I are back to discussing a healthy eating plan for a vigorous life.

"You have to keep God out of the equation," Mario rejoins. "I've read the Bible a couple of times, Albertina, and I remember the gospel of Luke when Jesus says, 'Do not worry about your life, as to what you will eat; nor for your body, as to what you will put on. For life is more than food, and the body more than clothing.' Well, if that's how the Savior feels, He's obviously not in the nutrition business."

"Please, Mario," I say, "you know as well as I that you're taking that Scripture out of context. The Lord goes on to say that God provides for everyone and everything, even the ravens. How can you, dear Mario, a lover of poetry, not love the lines in this same passage that say, 'Consider the lilies, how they grow: they neither toil nor spin; but I tell you, not even Solomon in all his glory clothed himself like one of these.' Jesus says, 'But seek His kingdom, and these things will be added to you.'"

"He's telling you to neglect the world," Mario argues.

"He *is* the world," I rejoin. "He's telling you to put first things first."

"Religion and healthy lifestyles do not mix."

"You keep calling it religion," I say. "Religion is a narrow word. But God is the living Word. He's the Word that gives all other words their meaning. There is no health, no true spiritual health, without tapping into the source of all health. The ultimate health is God."

"We're going around in circles," Mario declares.

"We're going around a track," I remind him.

"I'd like you to change tracks, Albertina. I'd like you to join me in a nutrition education program I'm designing to go out over the airwaves and into cyberspace—TV, satellite radio, Internet blogs, iPodCasts, the whole business."

"That sounds wonderful, Mario, but what purpose would I serve?"

"Black men will relate to me. Black women will relate to you. You're well known in our community."

"To a limited degree."

"You underestimate yourself, Albertina."

I don't reply. I'm feeling a little winded. I'm still building myself back up after the surgery. As our conversation has grown more intense, our pace has quickened.

"Let's relax for a second," I suggest.

"We'll relax for as long as you like," Mario graciously concedes.

We find a bench where we sit in silence for a while. After two or three minutes, Mario asks me if I'd mind if he reads me a sonnet by Shakespeare. "It's the thirtieth one," he says. "For me, the most exquisite."

When to the sessions of sweet silent thought
I summon up remembrance of things past,
I sigh the lack of many a thing I sought,
And with old woes new wail my dear time's waste:
Then can I drown an eye, unus'd to flow,
For precious friends hid in death's dateless night,
And weep afresh love's long since cancell'd woe,
And moan the expense of many a vanish'd sight:
Then can I grieve at grievances foregone,
And heavily from woe to woe tell o'er
The sad account of fore-bemoaned moan,
Which I new pay as if not paid before.
But if the while I think on thee, dear friend,
All losses are restored and sorrows end.

He recites the lines with such tender feeling that I can't help but be moved. Underneath his lovely reading, though, is a tinge of regret. I ask him what it's about.

"It'll be easier for me to explain if we can take a little drive," he says. "Do you mind?"

"Not at all."

A mile or two down Martin Luther King Boulevard, not far from the Crenshaw Mall, we take a detour down a side street and park in front of a community garden. Mario opens the car door for me—he's always a gentleman—and offers his hand. We slowly walk through the garden. The aromas are delicious—fresh herbs, cabbage, carrots, radishes, tomatoes, onions, peppers, and peas in various stages of growth.

"This garden has been here for years," says Mario. "As you know, it's not even a mile from my house. Until I had my heart attack and Blanche passed, I never paid it any mind. Not for a second. Oh, I'd pass it by and think it was quaint. But I never understood its meaning. I was too wrapped up in my own agenda."

I was sick of working for the man and dead set on making it on my own. The man was not only the television network executive who controlled my fate, but the man was also my father whose shadow had been haunting me my whole life. So I wasn't going to work in TV and I wasn't going to run a fancy restaurant. I'd cook for my own people in my own neighborhood and that would be that. I'd keep it simple. Eggs and bacon. Ham and eggs. Flapjacks. Sausages. Cheeseburgers for lunch. Fried chicken for dinner. Cornbread, biscuits, apple cobbler. I'd be a short-order cook, but the best in human history. I'd own the place, I'd run the place, I'd answer to no one. And I did. But what did I do?

"Albertina, I don't have to tell you that I didn't give one thought to nutrition. Not one. I gave the people what they wanted, what *I* wanted, what we were used to. I fell into our habits. And in the most personal way imaginable, through the loss of Blanche and my heart attack, I discovered those habits are deadly."

He bends down to touch a head of leafy lettuce.

"Feel this," Mario says. "This is real. If you look at food—real food, fresh food—if you open your eyes to the reality of food, your perception changes. If you read about it, as I've been doing since all this sickness, you understand how this fast-food culture corrupts us in a million ways. We're drowning ourselves in a sea of grease and fatty oils. We're killing ourselves on supersized portions of sugar and salt. We're eating ourselves to death. That was me only a few months ago. I was cooking it. I was serving it. I was eating it. I was part of the problem. Now I need to be part of the solution. The problem touched you when your gallbladder failed. It touched Justine when she suffered a heart attack. Eventually it'll touch all of us if we don't wake up. I need to wake up the people. Don't you see, Albertina. I need your help. And, to be honest, I don't see how you can refuse. I don't see how your sense of doing God's will, whatever that may be, could not convince you that this work is urgent and absolutely necessary, right here and now."

Circumcision of the Heart

Right here and now, in the middle of September, two big meetings are coming up. Both are challenging. The first is with Rabbi Cohen's congregation, the second with our own church members to make a final decision about whether to sell.

Patrick is leading the faith exchange meeting tonight between our church and Naomi's temple. Naomi has said at least thirty members of her congregation will be coming to our sanctuary. When I told her that Patrick would be speaking in my place, she asked, "At your suggestion?" "No," I replied, "at the suggestion of the Holy Spirit." Naomi did not seem displeased. In fact, she and Patrick have spoken about the topic and settled on the concept of circumcision seen from Old and New Testament points of view. It's nice to know that they're talking again.

On the way home I stop by Justine's to see how she's doing. She comes to the door in an oversized sweatshirt with the words FORMER PHAT GIRL written across the front.

"You caught me on the bike," she says. "I was sweating to the oldies."

"That's good, baby. The oldies will get you moving."

"Want some herb tea? I've given up coffee."

"Don't want to disturb your workout, Justine."

"Workout's done. Come on in."

Passing through the living room, where Justine has positioned her exercise bike in front of the TV, I can't help but notice a DVD of *Walker's Wonder Program of Mental and Physical Health.*

Justine sees that I've spotted it.

"He sent it to me," she confesses. "It's the new version. Your daughter-in-law is in it."

"I know."

"I can't help but sneak a peek at it now and then. The man is so fine."

"I thought you swore never again to have anything to do with him."

"I get bored exercising, Albertina. Everyone does. He keeps me interested. He and I have some interesting memories."

"What I remember, Justine, is the pain he inflicted upon you."

"He's a good-for-nothing playa, that's for sure."

"Why did he send this to you?"

"He's apologizing. Feels terrible for what he did to me. He heard about my little heart attack and wants to help me get back in shape."

"And you don't think he has an ulterior motive?"

"I know he does. I'm just curious to see what it is. Two can play this game."

To my eyes, the couple standing in the pulpit of the House of Trust look like they belong together. They are exceptionally good-looking and well-groomed. My nephew Patrick is a few inches taller than Rabbi Cohen. His eyes are brown; hers are green. Their medium-brown skin tone is about the same. Patrick is wearing a blue blazer and gray slacks. Naomi is wearing a gray pin-striped skirt and black blouse. They each have a professional demeanor, a seriousness about them that adds to their allure. I see them as a man and woman of God. Sitting in the first pew, surrounded by members of both my congregation and Rabbi Cohen's, I'm delighted that they are making this joint appearance. The church is packed.

Naomi begins by explaining the reasoning behind male circumcision. She speaks softly but with great clarity and self-assurance. Circumcision is a commandment, she says, given in the Bible, a sign of a holy covenant: On the eighth day of a boy's life, the foreskin of his penis must be removed. Circumcision symbolizes a commitment to God etched in blood. The sign is unalterable. There can be no mistake about a Jewish man's loyalty to his Lord. He is set apart.

When Naomi is through, Patrick begins. He too speaks in measured tones and with scholarly confidence. He points to the famous passage in Romans 2:29, which says, "circumcision is that which is of the heart, by the Spirit, not by the letter." He talks about how Jesus' ethos of love transcends the older ethos of Talmudic law. "The symbolism of circumcision," he explains, "remains intact. We must give of ourselves to God. But the circumcision is mystical rather than literal."

"There is great continuity," adds Naomi, "between the culture of the Old Testament and the New."

"Great continuity," Patrick adds, his tone growing somewhat tense, "but also great divergence. The New Testament says one no longer has to be circumcised to belong to God. One has to merely confess that Jesus Christ is Lord and Savior."

"The symbolism may shift," says Naomi, looking for an area of agreement, "but the meaning is the same. We must humble ourselves before God. We must recognize His awesome majesty and divine goodness."

"We must look to Christ for salvation or face doom," states Patrick, his voice rising.

Naomi doesn't respond. The members of her congregation are visibly shaken.

"You may not want to hear it," says Patrick, "but there's no reason to avoid the issue. Christ is Lord. Christ is the name we put above all others. There is no way to the Father other than through Him. There is no spiritual compatibility between those who accept that unchanging idea and those who reject it. Accept it and you are saved. Reject it and you are damned."

Naomi is stunned. I am stunned. Patrick is unyielding. His eyes are filled with righteous indignation. He leaves the pulpit. Naomi is standing alone. She doesn't know what to say.

I go to the pulpit and say a short prayer, invoking the God who loves us all as His children, but the prayer comes too late. The damage has been done. Our Jewish guests feel like they've been ambushed and insulted. Rabbi Cohen leaves without saying a word.

"If this is how you're comporting yourself tonight, Patrick," I ask, "what behavior can I expect from you when we bring up the issue of relocation?"

"You won't have to worry about that, Aunt Albertina, because I won't be there. I'm resigning from the House of Trust."

part Two

The wind blows where it wishes and you hear the
sound of it, but do not know where it comes from
and where it is going; so is everyone who
is born of the Spirit.

—JOHN 3:8

Megachurch Moguls

"What do you mean Patrick quit?" asks my son, Andre, who's calling me at my church office from New York. "He can't quit. He's your nephew. You're the reason he's a minister. You're his inspiration, Mom."

"Well, baby, seems like I've inspired him to move on."

"To where?"

"Satellite Fellowship of Faith Church."

"What? The people who are trying to move you out?"

"The very same, sweetheart."

"That's infuriating! You must be beside yourself."

"I have feelings about it, but I wouldn't say fury is one of them."

"Oh come on, Mom. You must be angry."

"Disappointed, but deep in prayer."

"Praying that Patrick will come back to the fold?"

"No, praying Ephesians 4:32 where it says, 'Be kind to one another, tender-hearted, forgiving each other, just as God in Christ also has forgiven you.'"

"So you admit he needs forgiveness."

"We all do, baby."

"Well, I'm never talking to him again," says Andre. "And I know Laura will feel the same."

"Patrick needs time, Andre."

"Time for what?"

"To sort things out. To grow and find himself."

"Meanwhile, he's scheming with those megachurch moguls to kick you out."

"I'm not being kicked out that fast."

"Do you have a game plan, Mom?"

"No, but God does."

"And we have no idea what it is, do we?"

"Not yet."

"I wish I knew God's career plan for my wife," Andre says with a sigh.

"I thought Nina was doing well."

"Too well. She's been on the road more than she has been home. Now she's in the Bahamas shooting another one of those infomercials."

I want to ask whether it's with Walker Jones, but I don't. I get the feeling that Andre appreciates my silence.

After our chat, just as I start preparing for Bible class, my assistant Denise hands me a FedEx overnight letter. It's from the Adams Boulevard Business Association. In polite but no uncertain terms, the organization argues that House of Trust must sell for the betterment of the community. Not to do so, they imply, would be unchristian. The letter carries the signature of some forty merchants in the area.

Not two hours pass before Denise comes into my office again, this time with a certified letter from my local councilman. "For the good of all," he writes, "relocating House of Trust would be of great service."

I file the second letter with the first.

I say a little prayer and pick up the phone to do what I should have done weeks ago: I call my lawyer.

Encounter

Encounter is a space age–style restaurant designed to look like the old *Jetsons* TV show. It sits atop the old air traffic tower at Los Angeles International Airport and offers a perfect view of planes coming and leaving. Bob Blakey, my late niece's husband and the man I call my lawyer, has asked me to meet him here. He's traveling to Tokyo on business and has a layover. I refused Bob's kind offer to have a car and driver fetch me. I'm perfectly capable of driving myself.

I'm early for the meeting. The September sunset is spectacular, the sky glowing a golden blue as jets stream in and out. Watching the planes take off and land, I feel a rhythm, a movement, an unfolding of events, an unceasing choreography of change that, for some reason, calms and delights me. It's one of those God-is-in-the-heavens-and-all-is-right-with-the-world moments.

Bob arrives. He's an upbeat man with a burly build, clean-shaven head, and gleaming dark skin. His kind eyes smile from behind large gold-framed glasses. He's wearing a double-breasted blue suit, a fine white shirt, and a sun yellow striped tie.

We embrace.

"Glad we could squeeze this in, Aunt Tina," he says. "You look wonderful."

"Glad to see you're wearing the tie I sent you last month for your thirty-fifth birthday."

"Thirty-sixth," he gently corrects me.

"You hardly look thirty," I say.

"Before you say anything else, let's pray," he suggests. "I miss our prayers together."

We close our eyes and join hands. "Father God," I say, "thank You for Your eternal presence in our lives, Your presence in our hearts, Your presence in our souls. We just love You and honor You today, Lord. I thank You for Bob and the way he has blessed my life. I pray that You bless him and let his many talents continue to glorify You. Grant him traveling mercies, dear Lord, and unyielding trust in You. May others see Your handiwork in him, Father God, and be inspired by his loving heart. In the precious name of Jesus, Amen."

"I love when you pray, Aunt Tina," says Bob. "I wish you could pray with me every day."

"You have Him," I say, "and He's all you need."

"I need to slow down, that much I know," says Bob. "A good practice in entertainment law is a blessing, but right now I'm feeling over-blessed."

"Not that it's my business, Bob, but are you leaving room for a personal life?"

"That life ended with Cindy," he says.

My niece Cindy died last year at age thirty of cancer. Bob married her while she was in the hospital, only days before her passing.

"I miss Cindy every day," I say, "but I know your life will continue to be showered with blessings, Bob. Blessings you can't even imagine."

"Let's talk about your life, Aunt Tina, and this megachurch business."

"Go right ahead," I urge.

"Since you called," says Bob, "my staff and I have had time to do research. Financially, Bishop Gold and his Fellowship of Faith are the Exxon of evangelical Christianity—and that's saying a lot. Their resources are deep and their business dealings impeccable. In Dallas, where they've bought large parcels of land, they've consistently and intentionally paid over market price. They're more than fair. When they have expanded their church facilities—adding on an enormous gymnasium, school, and concert hall—they have employed the top construction firms and, in every instance, set higher than normal wage standards. Not only has Bishop made it a point to do business on the up and up, but he seems determined to act honorably in all his dealings."

"So the deal he's offering us is highly legitimate."

"Beyond legitimate, Aunt Tina. Desirable and lucrative. His real estate lawyers are among the most reputable in the country."

I sigh and take a moment to glance out the window. Night has fallen. The airfields are alive with blue and white lights flickering like fireflies.

"So is this famous offer one I can't refuse?" I ask.

Bob laughs. "Not at all. House of Trust owns the building and the land it sits on. No one can make you move."

"You've seen the petitions from the business community and council members?"

"I have. They're strong statements. I realize there's great pressure on you, Aunt Tina."

"Only if I allow that pressure to exert itself," I say. "Only if I refuse to offer that pressure up to God."

Bob and I order a light dinner and, for the next hour or so, share beautiful memories of Cindy.

I'm home by eight and in bed by ten. I dream of my mother. She's holding me in her arms, rocking me to an old song about the rugged cross. We're on a boat crossing a river. The waters are calm. Now instead of Mama holding me, I'm holding her. I'm a grown woman and Mama is frail. We're riding on a train, seated in a private compartment. Rain batters the windows, lightning streaks the sky. Mama is breathing her last breaths.

"Baby," she says, "are you saved?"

"I am, Mama."

"Have you been baptized in the holy water of His salvation?"

"I have, Mama."

"Do you know Him, child?"

"I do."

"Then you have nothing to fear."

Now we are flying, flying over rooftops, flying over vast snow-covered mountains, flying over still lakes and raging rivers.

Now we are young women—Mama and I—smiling at each other, walking down a path in a park fragrant with blooming flowers, on an afternoon of sunshine and serenity.

"You're free," says Mama, gently squeezing my hand. "Forever free."

I wake up, tears streaming down my face.

Before and After

When my baby Darryl was a little boy, he loved watching those crazy wrestlers on TV. He was a small-boned child who was forever drawing pictures of giants and huge monsters. He suffered because of his size and as a young teenager began taking vitamins and supplements to bulk up. I remember how he used to clip ads showing the before-and-after pictures of men who tried these muscle formulas. Before, the men were puny; after, they were big. But my son never felt he moved beyond the "before" stage. No matter how I tried, I couldn't convince him that God's love for us manifests itself in ways that transcend the appearance of the physical form.

I mention this to Mr. Mario as we walk through a farmer's market close to the Watts Towers in the heart of South Central L.A. Mario has just asked about Patrick and his sudden resignation.

"Patrick and Darryl had that before-and-after syndrome in common," I say. "Before Patrick came to Christ, he always yearned to be something he wasn't—a tough guy who could intimidate people. Patrick's dad, my husband Arthur's brother, was an intimidator. He ran a construction crew and was a strict and controlling boss. He had no room for religion or insubordination. He was a frightening man. He raised Patrick alone—his wife disappeared and we never knew why—and Patrick tried his best to keep up with dad. When I married Arthur, Patrick was a little boy and he took to me. I adored him. He followed my music and then he followed me into the ministry. I was thrilled that he gave His life to God, but at the same time I could still feel that his spirit of rebellion remained bottled up inside him. He was afraid to express himself with his dad, who could be moody and violent."

"In the second *Henry VI* play," says Mario, "Shakespeare talks about 'the spirit of putting down kings and princes.' That's not a bad spirit for us to embrace since kings and princes can deny our freedom and ability to declare our own identity."

"Our identity is in Christ."

"*Your* identity, sweet Albertina, not mine."

"Patrick's identity is surely in God."

"From all you've told me, Patrick is confused about his identity. Maybe he's tired of being seen as his aunt's assistant. Maybe he'll find a more satisfying identity with a big church that'll give him a big title, big responsibility, and maybe even big money. Those megachurches, all created in the name of the fallen God—"

"Risen God," I correct him.

"Fine, all those corporate-styled churches created in the name of the risen God you worship prove that this gospel of prosperity, no matter how corrupt the concept, is catching on like gangbusters. If Patrick wants in on that action—and that's his way of rebelling against his aunt's modest ministry—so be it."

I'm frustrated and want to respond, but I just shake my head instead. Mario is impossible and I refuse to be drawn into his fire. Besides, his mind has moved on. He's now squeezing tomatoes. He's carefully selecting fresh fruits and vegetables. He's been experimenting with new recipes and talking about writing a cookbook, opening a new restaurant, and producing a cable TV show. He's determined to get out his health message.

I'm determined to enjoy this Saturday. I love walking in the shadow of the Watts Towers. Constructed of makeshift rods of steel, wire, broken glass, seashells, and scraps of dishes, tiles, and ceramics, the work was fashioned by an Italian immigrant out of gratitude for his adopted country. I see the towers as glorious church spires, a monument to the God whose spirit is eternal hope.

"I'm just hoping," says Mario, dropping a few avocados into his shopping bag, "that this megachurch business will finally convince you that organized religion, like organized crime, is up to no good."

"Dear Mario," I reply, "God can be nothing *but* good."

"Good or not, Albertina, I wish I could help you with this megachurch problem you have, I really do, but I'm afraid I'm at a loss."

Dear Aunt Albertina

Dear Aunt Albertina,

I'm writing to apologize for the abrupt manner in which I tendered my resignation. Emotion overcame me in that moment, and I regret hurting or embarrassing you. I was upset because I felt the gospel of Christ being compromised—or, even worse, unspoken—at a moment when the Good News required direct and unapologetic declaration. I wish I had handled the situation more tactfully. Please forgive me, Aunt Albertina. I trust you will. You of all people know that my passion for Christ is real and right.

On the other hand, after days of reflection, I feel that my decision, no matter how intemperately expressed, is the right one. I have always respected your devotion to the Lord, but in recent months I cannot deny that differences in our spiritual outlooks have weighed on me. Let me be specific about two critical areas.

The first is our exchange ministry with Temple Abraham. My calling, short and simple, is to bring souls to Christ. That is my purpose in life. It is the first thing on my mind in the morning and the last thing on my mind at night. It is the very reason I exist in this mortal form. When this exchange began, I trusted that that very motive, to save souls, was your motivation for developing a relationship with Rabbi Cohen. But as time went on, Aunt Albertina—and I say this with all due respect— I feel as though your resolve softened. Your developing friendship with the rabbi diverted your purpose. And our sacred mandate somehow got lost. Instead of preaching Christ, we were pretending that there is perfect compatibility between believers and nonbelievers. I can't help but feel that this was hypocritical. When my passion for the Lord cannot be expressed, my heart suffers, my soul cries out, and frustration haunts me until I have to say something. *Christ is Lord! Christ is Lord!* And the world must know it.

The second issue, of course, is your decision to resist relocation. In perfect candor, Aunt Albertina, I'm convinced your decision rests on sentimentality, not vision. It's understandable that you're attached to that old bank building because it's your first physical church. But I don't have to remind you that the physical is not our central concern. The spiritual is. And the Spirit tells me that if House of Trust is to grow as a community in Christ, that growth requires more land, more seats, and a building with the potential to expand. Those are ideas you reject, just as you reject the great benefits that a church of the magnitude of Fellowship of Faith will bring to South Central L.A. Not only will the community's economy be revitalized, but the power of Christ will be felt up and down these streets with a vibrancy sure to attract thousands. Thousands of souls will be touched, thousands of lives changed, thousands of people, young and old, brought into the kingdom.

That's why I cannot turn down this calling to serve at Fellowship of Faith. That's why I was not only flattered when Bishop Gold and Pastor Solomon asked me to join them in their sacred effort, I was compelled to say yes— yes to progress, yes to ever-expanding evangelism, yes to Christ.

In His precious name,
Patrick

Dear Patrick

Dear Patrick,

His name is indeed precious, and so is yours. I thank you for writing me and I wish you nothing but further blessings and deeper peace.

I have no doubt of your devotion to God and His ability to continue to lead you into a life of service.

You're a wonderful young man, Patrick, and I'm so proud to call you my nephew.

We are one in Christ Jesus,
Aunt Albertina

Cousin Ginger

I originally met Clifford Bloom at the home of Rabbi Naomi Cohen. He was a guest at a Passover Seder that Patrick and I attended. That's where Clifford first found out about House of Trust. That night he promised to visit our church. Not only did he visit, he joined. Since then, he has gone out of his way to help me in any way he can.

Clifford is hosting a small dinner party tonight at a family restaurant, Ming's, in the heart of Chinatown. He has invited Rabbi Naomi Cohen; Roger Stein, a producer for National Public Radio; and a young woman named Ginger, Naomi's first cousin.

Ginger looks like Naomi, same shade of brown skin, same smiling eyes, same well-spoken demeanor. Like Naomi, she dresses with quiet flair. And also like Naomi, she exudes confidence.

Roger is a Jewish gentleman in his forties, rail thin, John Lennon glasses, scholarly aura. I recognize him as one of the members of Naomi's congregation who attended the interfaith program at House of Trust when the unfortunate incident with Patrick took place.

"Roger has been a colleague of mine for several years," says

Clifford. "He's responsible for all those wonderful programs on urban issues."

"Good to meet you," I say.

"I very much enjoyed your visit to our temple earlier this year," says Roger. "You were great."

"Why thank you," I say. "It was a privilege."

No one mentions Patrick. And it's not clear to me whether Roger is Ginger's or Naomi's date—or neither's.

This is the first time I've seen Naomi since the incident, and, just to clear my mind, I say to her, "I'm still sorry about what happened at our church."

"You were in no way responsible for that," says Naomi, who is as sweet with me as ever. "No one blames you, Albertina. And the invitation for you to return to our temple still stands."

"Invitation accepted," I say.

"My dad is a big fan of yours," says Ginger. "He has your records and claims you're the most underrated soul singer of all time."

"That I'm rated at all," I reply, "is a source of mystery to me. Tell your dad he's a kind and generous man. Are he and Naomi's dad brothers?"

"They are," says Ginger. "They actually have an accounting firm together. And they're both deacons in the same church."

"Are you also a member?" I ask.

"No, I haven't been to church since I went off to college."

"Or temple," adds Naomi with a smile. "Ginger is the family atheist."

"Agnostic," Ginger corrects her. "I'm not saying God doesn't exist; I'm just saying that I don't know. And, if you good ministers forgive me for saying so, I don't especially care."

"Ginger," says Roger, "is a pragmatist."

"Roger should know," says Ginger. "We lived together for two years."

I take careful note of the past tense. I presume they're no longer a couple.

"Ginger," adds Clifford, "also holds a master's degree in urban planning from UCLA. I met her when Roger was doing a series on historic preservation of the West Adams District."

"That's where House of Trust is located," I say.

"I know," says Ginger. "I can't tell you how pleased I was when you restored the old bank building and kept the exterior virtually intact. Not to mention the beautiful paneling inside."

"So you've been to House of Trust?" I ask.

"Yes, several times."

"During services?"

"I'm afraid not, Pastor. I came by during the renovations, and on a morning after the work was done. Your secretary was kind enough to show me around. I loved what you did."

"Well, thank you."

"Ginger works as an urban resource consultant," says Clifford. "She advises large commercial property owners on how to maintain the historical integrity of their buildings. She's also the preservationist of the West Adams Historical Society. That's the organization dedicated to saving West Adams from destroying its unique architectural character."

"She's a zealot," says Roger Stein. "In the field of historical preservation, I call her an urban guerrilla."

"Roger's exaggerating," Ginger comments.

"I don't think so," says her cousin Naomi. "I don't think so at all. Change a doorknob in one of those old West Adams cottages and Ginger's ready to throw you in jail."

"Do you live in the neighborhood, dear?" I ask.

"I do, Pastor. I live on Arlington, not far off Adams."

"Not far from House of Trust," I observe.

"Three blocks away. I'd like to write about the transformation."

"You better hurry," says Clifford. "It may not be there by the time your article comes out."

"What!" Ginger exclaims.

Clifford explains the situation in detail.

"I had no idea," says Naomi. "I think that's outrageous."

"More than outrageous," says Ginger, "it's a slap in the face of our community. The preservationists won't stand for it."

"So you see, Albertina," says Clifford, "you have a few staunch supporters."

"We can work to get House of Trust into the National Register of Historic Places," Ginger offers. "Once that's accomplished, it'll take years for a developer to push you off the land. And chances are, he never will. Time delays and legal costs will scare him away. We'll find all sorts of ways to block him."

"I already have the best way," I say. "House of Trust owns the building *and* the land. We can stay put forever."

"Then what's the problem?" asks Ginger.

"The will of the congregation is unsettled," I say. "It's something I need to pray on."

"Will is a whimsical thing," adds Roger. "A lifetime in public relations and broadcasting has taught me the gentle art of persuasion."

"And are you willing to apply that art to our cause?" asks Clifford, who sees his job as galvanizing the troops and leading the battle. This, I now see, was his purpose in organizing this gathering.

"Sure," says Roger. "I like a good battle. And from personal experience I can tell you that Ginger does too."

Roger's last statement has an obvious subtext. But later in the evening, when Roger moves closer to Naomi and puts his arm around her, and when, in fact, at evening's end they leave the restaurant together, I realize that this situation—Clifford, Roger, and the two cousins—is far from a simple one.

Simple Truth

Jesus said it simply. "I am the light of the world; he who follows Me will not walk in the darkness, but will have the Light of life." It's all there in John 8:12. Clear as day. He is light; He is life.

So I'm believing Him. I'm following Him. I'm living in His Word. I'm keeping it simple.

But hard as I try, I can't always get the message of simplicity across to others. Case in point: Dear sweet Justine.

Dear sweet Justine is carrying on with two men at the same time.

We're at a stretching/aerobics class at a new gym we've joined on Venice Boulevard, not far from where we live. The teacher has gotten us all limber and loose and now we're riding stationary bicycles. Justine has dropped a bunch of weight and is finally getting into shape. We're sweating to the oldies—the Supremes are singing "Baby Love"—and, although Justine is a little winded, she's still capable of dishing the dirt.

"I don't think they mind sharing me," says Justine.

"Do they even know that they're sharing you?" I ask.

"No," she admits, "but if they did know they wouldn't mind."

"You're presuming."

"I'm having a ball. Besides, Clarence Withers is just an occasional drop-off-the-mail kind of thing."

I can't help laughing because now the tune "Please, Mr. Postman" is playing.

"I thought you really liked Johnny Marbee," I say.

"Love him. Johnny's a complete doll. He's my teddy bear. And this month he's our Target employee of the month."

"That's great."

"He gets a special parking place for thirty days. But I told him, I said, 'Johnny, you can park it with me wherever and whenever you wanna.' " Justine laughs at her own joke.

"This is serious business," I have to say. "You're going to wind up hurting one of these guys."

"Look, Tina, men have been doing it for years. One steady and one on the side. It's an easy game to play."

"But that's just the point," I reply, picking up speed on my bike, "you treat it like a game. You can't play with emotions. You can't play with men like they're toys."

Justine raises her eyebrows, looks at me like I'm crazy, and says, "I can't?"

"Not and stay in the Spirit."

"Well, honey, with my energy and my new figure, my spirit couldn't be any better. In fact," she says, eyeing a dark-skinned gentleman lifting weights in the corner, "my spirit is saying, 'Maybe two's too few.' "

There's no use in preaching to Justine. No use in lecturing. She knows how I feel. All I can do is live the life I live. If it inspires her, fine. If not, I tried.

To keep the life I lead simple is not a simple task. Simplicity, I know, rests in trusting God's love. I do that. But from time to time my human mind can trip. I can worry more than I need to. Worry about Laura in Chicago, worry about Andre in New York, worry about Justine next door, worry about Patrick wherever he is.

When I get home from the gym, I find another letter from Patrick, only this one is on the official stationery of Fellowship of Faith and he is listed as one of the half-dozen assistant pastors.

He tells me how happy he was to get my note, and how he appreciates my understanding. Then he goes on to say that he's taken an apartment in Dallas, home of Fellowship of Faith, but is also keeping his place here in L.A. Bishop Gold has put him in charge of the Fellowship of Faith transition team between Texas and California. I wonder: Does that mean that his job is to talk me into selling House of Trust? He doesn't say. Instead he lets me know that Bishop Gold himself will be in touch with me about an entirely different matter. "This is something that will excite you, Aunt Albertina, because it involves telling the Good News in an arena that to you will be like second nature." Patrick's tone is polite but a little brusque. I wonder what in the world Bishop has in mind for me. I don't have to wait long. The next morning, while I'm having my coffee and watching Maggie Clay interview Condi Rice, an overnight letter from the good Bishop arrives. It is, I admit, something I never would have expected in a million years.

Mega Joy

Nothing wrong with "mega." My old Webster's dictionary says it just means "huge" and "important." I'm not against the word. And I'm not against applying it to Jesus. He is mega. He is the One, the Alpha and the Omega. I'm believing John 14:6 when He says, "I am the way, and the truth, and the life."

But I confess that I'm a little cautious when I hear "mega" applied to churches and church conferences. Yet here I am, reading an extravagantly flattering letter inviting me to lead a seminar at the Mega Joy Christian Conference (MJCC) to be held in Dallas. My instinct is to say no. Isn't this simply a manipulation? A way to soften my position and get me to sell the church? Isn't this something to be avoided?

"You will be ministering to over a hundred of the most prominent women in our national community, including the Honorable Mayor of Chicago and the Honorable Governor of Georgia. I could think of no one, Pastor Merci, who exemplifies the spirit of Christ more than you. I know of no one who could better explain how God manifests Himself in every aspect of our personal and professional lives."

He goes on to say how Mega Joy will be providing me with first-class plane tickets, a suite at the Fairmont Hotel, and an extremely generous honorarium.

"I thank you in advance, my dear friend," Bishop concludes, "for joining me in this great crusade to give God glory and expand the reach of His marvelous message of eternal love."

When I read the words "my dear friend," I can't help but wonder. The judgmental part of my mind says the man is being hypocritical. Bishop Gold has never paid me any mind in the past. Why now? I am tempted to write him back and ask him that very question. But sarcasm is not my style. What's the point of making an accusation when he has offered me a podium that, in truth, I find attractive? There's no reason not to think about it.

But there's no time to think about it now because the phone rings and it's Rhonda Bolden, a parishioner of mine. Rhonda is an accomplished and educated young lady in her thirties. She is the principal of an elementary school. She and her partner, Lisa Adams, a high school history teacher, were kicked out of the church of their choice because of their sexual orientation. Patrick was fired from his position at that church for giving Rhonda and Lisa key roles in the church's education program. That's when he came to work with me—and I invited Rhonda and Lisa to join House of Faith. They joined, and controversy among our membership followed but, I'm proud to say, tolerance and love carried the day. Rhonda and Lisa have been accepted with warm gratitude as valuable members of our spiritual community.

Rhonda, the most composed of women, is crying her eyes out. I am shocked to hear her in such a state. Between her sobbing, I can hardly make out what she's saying. She's that upset.

"Let me just come over," I suggest.

Driving to the home she shares with Lisa in Baldwin Hills, an upscale neighborhood not far from my house, I wonder if the two women have had a falling out. I wonder whether this involves betrayal or abandonment.

My speculation is far off the mark.

Lisa is away in England at a teacher's conference, Rhonda

tells me when I arrive. Rhonda has calmed down a bit since our phone conversation, but her pretty brown eyes are still filled with tears. Her breathing is still irregular. The crisis has nothing to do with Lisa. Rhonda's aunt Lillian has died and her family in Atlanta has told Rhonda that she is not welcome at the memorial service or the funeral. Rhonda is covered with pain—pain over the death of her aunt, pain over the rejection she's feeling from her family.

"Lillian was my favorite aunt," she says in between sobs. "My mother could be cold and withdrawn, but Aunt Lil was all sweetness and light. She had no children of her own and cared for me and my brothers with more love than you can imagine. My own mother had mental health problems, Pastor. For months, even years, she was unavailable emotionally. When they finally took my mother away to a hospital, Aunt Lil came to live with us. She had enough maternal love for everyone. She really became our mother. When Mama recovered and came home, Aunt Lil stayed because for many more months Mama was confined to her room. The whole thing was frightening for everyone, but Lil made it all right. She spoke about God, Pastor, at a time when God wasn't spoken about in our house. She prayed openly. She took my hand and said, 'Now's let's just thank Him. Let's just praise Him. Let's just rejoice in His holy name.' Her prayers weren't fancy. They were plain prayers that went right to the heart of the matter. As I grew up, went to college, and forged a life of my own, Mama became even more distant while Aunt Lil became understanding of my life and work. She came to my college graduation. She was there when I received my master's in education. When Lisa and I became a family, Aunt Lil was our first dinner guest. She came all the way from Atlanta to see our place and bring a housewarming gift, a silver bowl her husband, Louis, had given her for their fiftieth wedding anniversary the year before he died. We loved the sentiment. We took it as approval of our relationship. Mama, meanwhile, broke off all ties when she learned I was committed to Lisa. So did my father and my uncles and aunts. Everyone except Lillian. She stood alone. And the great thing is that she never argued with them. She just kept being who she has always been—an aunt whose passion was to love, not judge.

"She'd been sick these past five years. Alzheimer's. Little by little, her mind turned cloudy and she was sometimes forgetful. But when Lisa and I visited her, her eyes lit up. She never failed to recognize us. Never failed to ask about us. Lillian was a most selfless person. It was all about how can I help *you*. You remind me of my aunt, Pastor. That's why I'm so glad you came over. That's why it hurt so bad when I was told that I would not be welcome at the memorial service or the funeral. I could go anyway and make a scene. But that would hardly honor Aunt Lil's quiet disposition. She never fought with anyone. So here I am, left out in the cold while my aunt is being remembered by people whose memories are far less loving than mine. How do you mourn when you're not allowed to mourn? When a family member passes on, you want to mourn with your family. That's when family is so important. You don't want to mourn alone."

"You're right, Rhonda. This is a time when family can comfort. Being surrounded by family is a blessing."

"And a curse when they banish you."

"No one is banished from the love of God. We mourn together as family, Rhonda. You and I mourn together as sisters in Christ; we mourn as mother and daughter; we mourn as an aunt and niece; we mourn as servants of our crucified God and we celebrate as believers in our risen God. We offer Him our hurt and pain, as He offers us His. His death is our life, and His life is in ours. He grieved and mourned and we do too. We weep. Jesus wept. We feel the sting of rejection, just as, time and again, He was rejected. We turn to Him for the hope that is His name, the love that is His character, and the forgiveness that is our salvation.

"We can thank God for Aunt Lil, and the years she nourished you, and the way she opened your heart, and the fact that she'll never leave because she lives with you. Her sweetness is part of who you are, Rhonda; her sweetness is her legacy to you. This is her memorial service, right now and right here, and this is her special gift to me, that I get to sit and pray with you, Rhonda. I get to know Aunt Lil through you. I get to feel all that is good and beautiful about her eternal soul."

Rhonda is crying again, holding on to me and crying. I know she feels alone. I know that her pain is acute. Her family's coldness is a slap in the face at a time when Rhonda hungers for their warm embrace. The pain stays. But so does the spirit of Aunt Lil.

It's always somewhat surprising to see a woman like Rhonda, a school principal who's normally so contained, out of sorts. It shows me that all of us, even the most controlled, have the hearts of little children. Those hearts can be broken so easily. And it's only God, I tell Rhonda, who can heal our hearts.

For a long time, we sit and pray together. When our prayers are concluded, I ask Rhonda if she'd like to have dinner. I hate for her to be alone this evening. She has schoolwork to attend to, she says, and assures me that she'll be fine.

"I can't thank you enough for coming," she says.

"Thank God," I say.

I decide to drive over to Whole Foods, pick up a little fresh fish and vegetables, and cook at home. On the way, I think of Rhonda's aunt Lillian and all the nameless women who, while not biological mothers, have served in that role and thus raised strong and wonderful children. I think of motherhood—and fatherhood— as a beautiful way of serving God. Aunt-hood, uncle-hood . . . when we mentor children, when we provide them with patience, understanding, and boundless love, we make them strong. I see Rhonda as a strong and good woman in the world. Thank you, Aunt Lillian.

These good thoughts are going through my mind as I'm

squeezing tomatoes at Whole Foods when I hear my cell phone ringing out the melody of "Precious Lord, Take My Hand." I don't like cell phones—they're intrusive—and, until I began pastoring House of Trust, I didn't have one. However, they're necessary in my line of service. It helps a little that my ringtone plays one of my favorite songs, but I can't say I'm happy to have my vegetable shopping interrupted.

It's Denise from church.

"Sorry to disturb you, Pastor," she says, "but Barbara Nile just called. Something terrible has happened. Her son Nelson has been murdered. I thought you'd want to know."

I ask Denise to give me the address of Barbara and her husband, Nelson, Senior. I ask her if she knows the circumstances. All Denise can tell me is that Nelson, Junior, a pastor who went to theology school with my nephew Patrick, was doing his work as a ride-along minister with the police when it happened. I thank Denise, put back the groceries I have selected, and head out to the Niles.

Barbara Nile, a paralegal for a large downtown law firm, and her husband, Nelson, a captain with the Los Angeles Police Department, live in Village Green, an apartment complex that was built on a beautiful expanse of green lawns back in the thirties. I met Barbara years ago when I was singing the blues. She worked for my music attorney, Morris Fogler, who has since passed. Barbara came to the Lord many years ago, and when she learned I had become a pastor she called to congratulate me. We talked for hours on the phone and next thing I knew she was attending Sunday morning services in my home. It took Nelson a while to join her, but he finally came around. I've known Nelson, Junior, since he was an infant.

Their apartment is covered in grief. Barbara is seated on a couch. She is weeping quietly. Embracing her, I can feel her shaking. She is rail thin and fragile as a leaf. She is unable to speak. We hold on to each other for a long while. Nelson is seated in a reclining chair, also speechless. He is not crying. He thanks me for coming over, then stares ahead. His eyes are vacant. I, too, stay silent. I sit on the couch next to Barbara and hold her hand. Many minutes pass before Nelson speaks.

"You know my son," he says. "You know his heart."

"Yes," I say.

"I thought he'd become a policeman," he continued. "He always wanted to. He'd come down to the station with me when he was a little boy and ask everyone every question imaginable. He has a beautiful mind and a beautiful curiosity. But you know what, Albertina? I prayed that he wouldn't join the force. I prayed that he'd find safer work. And when he found God, I rejoiced. I said, 'Thank you, Jesus. You've heard my prayer and You've answered it. You've called my boy to be Your servant. Glory!' I said, 'Glory Hallelujah!' And then you know what happened, Pastor. You know how he saw his service. He saw it serving people like me, his dad. He saw it serving the police, riding along with us so he could help us reach the helpless, the crazed, the criminals who might not respect us but just might respect him. And he's great at it, just great. He has a way with people, Albertina, he has a touch. People trust him. Everyone loves him. Everyone."

I want to ask how he came to be murdered, but I don't. I know that the best thing I can do is listen. Barbara is still holding my hand. Her sobbing is so deep I feel my heart breaking. Ten minutes later, her husband speaks again of their son.

"He was riding with Bub Phillips, a rookie cop, when they got a call about an altercation in a bar. They went there and Nelson saw the guy everyone called Bongo. Bongo and my son had gone to school together. Bongo had a long history of violence. This time he'd struck a man in the face and Bub was ready to haul him in, but Nelson said, 'Let me talk to him.' So Nelson got Bongo some coffee and sobered him up and calmed him down and maybe even ministered to him, I don't know. Nelson loved to minister to everyone. He never gave up on anyone. So Bongo did calm down, and Nelson got Bongo to agree to let him and Bub drive him home. Bub told me he was amazed at how Nelson had such a peaceful effect on people. They were driving Bongo home, and Bongo was actually praying with Nelson, asking God for forgiveness for all the bad stuff he'd done in his life. Bub told me the last thing Nelson said was, 'Bongo, His grace covers everything. You're already forgiven.' They pulled up to Bongo's house, where he lived with his mother, Bongo gets out and everything seems okay. But then Bongo—"

Here Nelson, Senior, has to stop. He breathes deeply and fights for composure before he continues.

"Then Bongo—" he tries again, but he can't say the words. Barbara's sobbing and shaking get worse.

"Then Bongo . . ." her husband goes on, "Bongo smashes Bub in the face, grabs his gun, and shoots Nelson, point-blank, through the skull."

Silence.

My shock is profound. I've never heard a story like this before. I've never seen a family this devastated. I know that words of comfort will not work. There are times when not only are words inadequate, words can make it worse. Clichés, even those rooted in truth, can trivialize the awful pain people are going through. Besides, I am so saddened and baffled by this story that the only thing I can do is continue to hold Barbara's hand and stay silent. After a long while, I whisper a short prayer, "Father God, stay with us in our grief, stay with us in our confusion, let us feel Your presence. In Jesus' name, Amen."

I go out and bring them back hot food. They haven't eaten in many hours. The food does them good. We sit in silence for another hour until I ask whether they'd like me to read a Psalm. They say yes.

"Lead me in your Truth," says David's Twenty-fifth Psalm, "and teach me, for you are the God of my salvation; for you I wait all the day."

The baby's name is Noah Simon Sinclair. The Sinclairs are first-time parents and new members of House of Trust.

The baby-naming service takes place the Sunday after the death of Nelson, Junior.

Our church prays for Barbara and Nelson, Senior.

And then I name the baby.

The gorgeous little boy is fast asleep when I say, "Bless him, Father, and make him grow strong in Your grace. Let him be a spiritual leader among his people and praise You all the days of his life."

I lean down and kiss his cheek. I embrace his parents, their eyes moist with tears and happiness, and think to myself, *This is the meaning of mega joy.*

Cowboy Stadium

I grew up in Dallas and my memories are bittersweet. Sweet because of my mama and daddy and the family I loved so deeply. Bitter because Dallas is where we buried my beloved niece Cindy. Bitter because of the ugly racism I encountered there as a young girl.

Today Dallas has become a sophisticated city. But back in the day it was no more progressive than Backwater, Alabama. The message was clear: If you were black, stay back.

It's not in my nature to stay back for anyone. I wasn't raised that way. After a painful first marriage, I got out of Dallas and made my way in the world, so when I return to Dallas, my heart overflows with lots of feelings. Sometimes I have trouble finding my emotional balance.

This trip to the Mega Joy Christian Conference is no different. I'm staying at the Fairmont Hotel, where last year I saw my daughter-in-law consorting with Walker Jones, the exercise salesman. Not a happy memory, and one I've chosen to keep to myself.

My pocket calendar tells me that today is October 1. I have thirty days to report to Bishop Gold—and to his son Solomon and my nephew Patrick—about our church's decision whether to sell or stay. But, in a strange sense, I'm not worried. It will be what it will be.

The phone rings to tell me that the car has arrived to drive me to Cowboy Stadium in Irving, Texas, home of the Dallas Cowboys football team, where the conference is taking place.

Outside the stadium are concession stands where people are selling barbecue, peach cobbler, and incense, and "Mega Joy Forever" booths are set up to sell Bibles. One stack of Bibles carries a sign that says SPECIAL MEGA JOY EDITION, 25% OFF. By the entrance to the stadium, a man is holding up vials and exclaiming, "Holy water, get your holy water! Straight from the Jordan River. Get your genuine Jesus-baptized holy water!"

Inside the stadium, in a circle surrounding the playing field, which is set up with thousands of folding chairs, there are still more booths, selling everything from CD sermons to gold chains and diamond crosses.

The Messiah we worship, I think to myself, *wore sandals, rode a donkey, and was homeless. The Messiah we worship talked about the meek inheriting the earth. He warned about losing ourselves in worldly possessions. He kicked the merchants out of the Temple. He died without a single possession. He died to set us free, forgive us our sins, and offer eternal life.*

The sound from the stage breaks my reverie and makes me happy. It's LaShun Pace, a beautiful contemporary gospel artist, singing "The Lord Will Make a Way."

I make my way closer to the stage so I can absorb more of the music and the Holy Spirit. The rhythm is up, the rhythm is right, the choir behind LaShun is shouting, the horns are harmonizing, the drummer is driving hard. As I'm walking toward the musicians, I hear a voice say, "Pastor Merci, we always seem to meet up in the right places."

I turn around and see Walker Jones standing in front of the most extravagant booth in sight. Meanwhile, LaShun is singing,

"For my good but for His glory." I want to listen to LaShun; I don't want to deal with Walker, but I also don't want to be rude.

"Good morning, Mr. Jones," I say.

"Walker," he corrects me. "Do you have a moment to look over my new line of Christian exercise DVDs and my Christian nutrition plan?"

"You'll excuse me, but I must run," I say, noticing the huge gold cross hanging from Jones's neck. The contrast between the cross and his too-tight black tank top displaying his muscles is noticeable. "I'm due to speak soon."

"I saw that on the schedule," he says, "and I'll be there. You're my favorite minister. Your sermons are always right on."

I don't believe Walker has heard any of my sermons, but I'm not about to bring that up. By now, several church ladies are looking him over and want to ask him questions about the DVDs.

"I'll catch up with you later, Pastor," he says.

"Fine," I reply.

But I do not feel fine.

I proceed to a VIP area where I am escorted to an enormous dining room atop the stadium usually reserved for VIP ticket holders. Today the room is overflowing with women who have come to hear me. I can't help but be flattered. I recognize many of them as important civic and political leaders. My topic, in fact, is spiritual leadership.

Bishop Gold himself introduces me in terms that make me blush. He overstates my accomplishments and credentials. He makes it sound like I'm far more important than I am. He practically gushes. When he is through, the women give me a standing ovation. All this before I say a word.

I thank the Bishop and start with a prayer.

"Father God," I say, "may You inform our words and form our hearts to conform with Yours.

"Spiritual leadership sounds like a heavy subject," I start off saying, "but I want to keep it simple. To be honest, I don't see myself as a leader as opposed to one who is led. I'm led by Christ. He's the only leader I recognize and the only leader I need. Look to Him and You'll know where to go. Lose Him and you yourself are lost.

"I want to briefly say something about my life before I let Christ lead me. As you know, I was a singer. I loved singing and I loved show business. It's exciting to fly around the world with famous entertainers and stay at fancy hotels. It's exciting to look out and see thousands of people applauding what you do onstage. It's heady stuff.

"Every group, of course, has a leader. Ray Charles, for example, was a good leader. He was all business. The leader sets the tone for everyone else. I responded to the leader because I was a good follower. I wanted to do well and fit in. We all do. That's only natural.

"My story isn't as dramatic as the stories of others who followed certain leaders into drinking or drugging. I have better sense than that. But that doesn't mean that in other ways I wasn't a follower. I was. I didn't realize then—as I do now—that my connection to the Holy Spirit is the only force that can lead me to where I want to go. The pressure of my daily situation—that I was an entertainer who had to please Mr. Ray Charles—overrode everything else. I was a people pleaser of the highest order.

"I want people to like me. I'm uncomfortable when they don't. I like them to confirm my worth and validate my presence. That's just my nature. But when I came to the Lord, I saw that that was more than my nature. That was my obsession. And on some level, ladies, that was my spiritual malady. I was deriving my sense of self-worth from other people, not from God. I was being led by my insecurities, not my security that Christ died for my sins and gifted me with His boundless love. Today my worth is derived from Him. The world might accept me on a Monday and reject me on a Tuesday. The world sure rejected Him. But, like He said, His kingdom isn't of this world. This world can reject you, and often does, but He won't.

"So this business of leadership, like all things, comes back to Him. Whether we're cooks in the kitchen or CEOs in the boardroom, we can look to the one leader whose lessons are clear as a bell. We must lead with patience. Lead with kindness. Lead with compassion and understanding. Lead others by example. Lead others, as you have been led, back to the source of goodness and grace. Lead with your heart and you will lead others to Him. That's our blessing, our mandate, our gift, and our glory."

It's good for two standing ovations. The women seem genuinely moved by the words God has given me. One by one, they come up to me afterward, which is when I realize there's another agenda here, one I'm just beginning to understand.

"I'm Belinda Havery," says a young woman in her thirties. "I'm vice president for the Bank of America's Inner City Building Program for Los Angeles. We've joined up with Bishop Gold's Satellite Fellowship of Faith on Adams Boulevard. We'll have a small branch, right next to the church, and we just want you to know how happy we are to have you as an important part of our program."

I'm not sure what that means, and I'm not sure this is the time to ask, so I don't.

"Pastor Merci," says another woman who looks to be in her fifties. "You gave a beautiful Word today, and we look forward to working with you in Los Angeles. My name's Angela Booth, and I'll be setting up the Fellowship of Faith recording studio in our new facilities in L.A. I don't know if Bishop told you, but it will be state-of-the-art. The first thing we want to do is have you record with our choir. Bishop wants us to distribute a Pastor Merci gospel album all over the country. He's really excited about the project and tells me that you are too."

I smile and thank her for coming. The picture is becoming clear.

The woman who will be the head of Fellowship of Faith Drama Center says something similar to me. Her understanding is that I will use my background in show business to help with Fellowship of Faith's religious productions in L.A. Her assumption is that my church will be razed, the new megacomplex will be built, and all will be well. But, come to think of it, I'm not even sure these women have been told that my church stands in the way. All I know is that they assume we're all working together. They assume harmony and cooperation. Surely that's Bishop's strategy: for me to address a group of lovely ladies who presume we're one big happy family. That way, were I to decide to keep House of Trust in place, I would have bonded with a large group of people whose plans I'd be destroying. The burden of guilt would be on me.

Just when I think I understand the full extent of Bishop's plan, a woman named Robin Brown introduces herself to me as the Fellowship of Faith nutritionist and head nurse.

"Pastor," she says, "I'm delighted to meet you and delighted to learn that you've been working with Mr. Mario on his plan to disseminate information on healthy eating to our community."

I'm taken aback.

"Are you a friend of Mr. Mario's?" I ask.

"I haven't had the pleasure of meeting him, but I do know the publisher who's considering his book. The publisher is a close friend of Bishop's. In all candor, a recommendation from Bishop will almost certainly mean that the book will be published."

I'm astonished. How in the world did Bishop know about Mario's health crusade? And how did Bishop know about Mario's friendship with me? Was it Patrick who told him? Are they spying on me? Or is the megachurch's networking so intricate and vast that nothing escapes them? I'm feeling both impressed and compromised at the same time. I value my privacy. And suddenly here's a gargantuan organization that knows everything about me. It's ridiculous, but it's real. And even worse, Bishop's tactics are seductive and subtle. He brought me here to meet these ladies who have offered me nothing but admiration and respect. He has manipulated me into a tight spot. If I stick to my position and don't give up the church, I'll disappoint an army of women whom he has carefully cast as my supporters. It's bizarre. It's bewildering. It has my mind spinning in five different directions at once.

I leave the Mega Joy lovefest with a mega headache. A car takes me back to the Fairmont Hotel. I try to nap, but sleep won't come. I pray, *Father, take this confusion from my head and let me just be with You. Let me be with Your pure love and Your unconfusing grace. Let me keep it simple, Father. Let me just accept this experience as a fellowship in Christ. I don't have to jump ahead, Father. I don't have to analyze. Things will unfold as things will unfold. Let me stay steady in my dependence on You. Your wisdom is in me. Your wisdom is simple. Your wisdom says, 'Love these people. Love extravagantly. Follow love wherever love leads.' In Jesus' precious name, Amen.*

Love seems to lead me to call for a cab. I ask the cabbie to drive me to the neighborhood where I grew up, close to the old airport, Love Field. It's early evening, a cool and pleasant night. The area is still African American, still working folk. I get out of the cab in front of my old house. It has been repainted a fresh coat of white. It's more a cottage than a house, two tiny bedrooms, a small living room and kitchen. My brothers Fred and Calvin, both gone, shared one bedroom. My parents were in the other. I slept on the couch. I didn't mind. I love the feeling of family, and I felt protected in that house. Daddy protected us. He protected us all. Mama was a praying woman who sang of Jesus night and day. Now I see a young mother and two young children walking out the front door. She sees me standing there.

"I used to live here when I was a child," I explain.

"Would you like to come in and look around?" she offers. "The house is a little messy but we just did it over. My husband did it himself. He works construction."

"That's kind of you, sweetheart," I say. "I'd love to look around."

Inside, her husband is sitting on a couch in the living room, reading the Bible. His wife explains who I am. He is as cordial as she is. Their children, both girls, are adorable.

"When did you live here?" he asks.

"Long ago," I say. "Way back in the forties."

"Well, please make yourself at home," he says. "We love this house. It has good vibes."

"Beautiful vibes," I add.

"Was the Church of the Nazarene here when you lived here?" he asks.

"Certainly was," I say. "That's where Mama took us. It's where I first learned to love the Lord."

"Are you a preacher?" asks the woman.

"I am. Out in L.A."

"We go to the Church of the Nazarene. That's where Marianne and I both got saved," says the husband whose name is Norm David.

"My mother lives in L.A.," says Marianne. "She's out there right now in the hospital. I want to go to her but I can't. She's having heart surgery tomorrow. Will you pray for her, Pastor? Can we pray together?"

My heart jumps at the chance. To pray for others in the home where Mama taught me to pray—there's nothing I'd rather do.

"What's your mother's name?" I ask.

"Maureen."

We join hands and pray for Maureen. We pray long and hard. We pray everything that is in our hearts. We pray that Christ will expand our hearts to let us pray more. And we do pray more. Norm and Marianne and I pray for a good half hour, each of us speaking to the Lord and asking that His presence be felt mightily by Maureen.

"If you'll tell me the hospital where she's staying," I say, "I'll visit her tomorrow."

"You'd do that?" asks Marianne.

"I'd love to," I say.

"It's not an imposition?" asks Norm.

"It's my ministry. And my ministry is a blessing."

"Would you join us for dinner, Pastor?" asks Marianne. "That would be a blessing for us."

I accept and find myself in the bosom of a family I feel I've known my whole life. I feel as if Norm and Marianne are my children. I feel the spirit of Mama and Daddy, the spirit of my childhood, the Holy Spirit that infuses our lives with meaning and continuity.

I have dinner in the long-ago past and I have dinner in the here-and-now present. I have peace of mind all throughout dinner. Norm drives me back to my hotel.

"God has brought you to us," he says when I get out at the Fairmont.

"God brings us all things good and great," I reply.

Julius Caesar

"The play," says Mr. Mario, "is all about intrigue and manipulation. Remember in act two when Cassius refers to Mark Antony as 'a shrewd contriver'? Well, he might as well be referring to the great Bishop Henry Gold."

Mario and I are having a cup of tea in a pleasant coffeehouse in Leimert Park, the artsy district just off Crenshaw Boulevard in South Central L.A. We've just come from an open-air production of *Julius Caesar* that Mario directed. He used local college kids majoring in drama and did a marvelous job molding them into the roles. They wore street clothes, not costumes, and a couple of the actors—the boys who played Caesar and Cassius—were fabulous.

"As a people," Mario said before the show, "our verbal skills are off the hook. Look at the preachers. Look at the rappers. If Snoop Dogg can lead his disciples into the Dogg Pound, I can lead them into Shakespeare. If you want verbal fireworks—as our young people seem to crave—my man Shakespeare can give you all you can handle."

Mario had done himself proud. His actors burned through *Julius Caesar* with the skill of professionals.

"*Caesar*, you see," Mario is now explaining, "turns on man's ability to use language to persuade, convict, and compel. Clever language is the key to the play. That's just how the good Bishop is convicting and convincing you, my dear Albertina."

I love attending plays with Mario because he has so much to say that's interesting and insightful. And of course the last thing in the world I want to do during these occasions is argue with him. Besides, there's a good chance he's right. Maybe Bishop is like Cassius. It's hard to see his maneuvers to get me to move out as anything other than cunning.

On that very point, I've been meaning to tell Mario what I learned at the Mega Joy ballyhoo in Dallas—that Bishop wants to involve him in a health crusade conducted by the church. In exchange, Bishop will use his influence with his publisher friend to make sure Mario's book is published. When I approach the subject, Mario takes a sip of his green tea, smiles broadly, and says, "I've been wondering when you were going to bring that up."

"So you know about it?"

"I was called by the man himself. The great Bishop Gold."

"When did this happen?" I ask.

"Just after you got back from Dallas."

"And you didn't mention it to me?"

"I thought it was a subject more suitable for an in-person encounter."

"What did he tell you? I'm dying to know."

"The same thing that the devil told your Jesus: That the world, my friend, can be all yours for the asking if you just believe in me."

"How did you respond?"

"How do you think I responded?"

"With some cynicism," I guessed.

"I quoted Shakespeare, Albertina. I said, 'Bishop, as Brutus said when Caesar fell, "ambition's debt is paid." ' "

"And what did he say to that?"

" 'Explain yourself, Mr. Mario,' he said. 'I'm not sure I grasp your meaning.'

" 'Well, your meaning is clear, kind sir,' said I. 'You'd pay me to sell out my friend. What Antony said of Caesar, I say to you: "Ambition should be made of sterner stuff." '

" 'I'm trying to help you with your noble project,' said Bishop.

" 'Nobility,' I replied, 'has nothing to do with religious institutions who model themselves after profit-hungry corporations and do anything to anyone who stands in the way of their so-called progress. "Nobility" is a term reserved for the wise and the compassionate, the high-minded and the altruistic. You, sir, do not fit any of those descriptions. I decline your offer and respectfully request that you and your minions never approach me again.'

"And with that, dear Albertina, I hung up."

"You were rude to the man," I say.

"Extremely," Mario replies, smiling broadly.

"I'm sorry it came to that."

"I'm not," says Mario. "I relished the confrontation. My only regret is that I wasn't forceful enough. There are a couple of other choice names I could have called him. My contempt could have been expressed more extravagantly and effectively."

"Sounds like you did a pretty good job."

"So you approve after all," he says.

"No, I don't. You can disagree with the man and respectfully say so. No need to insult him."

"But it was so fun."

"You're impossible," I say.

"Oh, come on, Albertina. You secretly love what I did, don't you? You've been wanting to tell the old geezer to get lost for months. And besides, you like knowing that your true friends are loyal. I can find my own publisher without the help of some jackleg preacher. He and his grand schemes can go straight to—"

"I do appreciate loyalty, Mario, but I'm also not convinced that your plan to spread important health information to our community would not have been aided by accepting Bishop's offer."

"Me joining forces with a megachurch? Please, my dear, I'd sooner join the Republican Party."

"Helping people is helping people," I say. "Bishop is a master communicator."

"I can't believe you're talking this way, Albertina. I would have thought you'd be thrilled to hear how I told him off. I did it for you."

"I'm not questioning your motives, Mario. All I'm saying is that your goal is a good one—to help our people start eating right—and you need to think long and hard about how to achieve it."

"Even if achievement requires that I partner with the devil?"

"Bishop is hardly the devil."

"He's devilish in his ambition."

"What proof do you have of that?"

"Look at his lifestyle. He has a house the size of Dodger Stadium, a yacht, a private jet, a fleet of limos. You've seen the spreads in *Ebony*."

"I'm not one to judge a man by his possessions."

"Wasn't it your Jesus who said it's easier for a camel to pass through the eye of a needle than for a rich man to pass through the gates of heaven? Wasn't your Jesus a man without possessions? Didn't he live the life he preached by eschewing the traps of materialism? Wasn't his entire focus on the spiritual and not the material?"

"Sounds to me, Mario, like you've been loving on Jesus."

"Not in the least. Jesus is a fairy tale, but if you believe the tale, as Bishop purports to, for God's sake don't live like a king wearing a crown of gold. Bishop's Savior wore a crown of thorns."

"Bishop has done some good work."

"I can't believe you're defending the man, the same man who underhandedly is pushing you off your land."

"He's not pushing me off; he's offering an extremely handsome price to buy the land."

"You're hopeless, Albertina, you truly are. A snake has entered your garden and you see him as the bluebird of happiness. What naïveté!"

"Bishop Gold's ministries are effective. He has reading-enhancement programs for children, teens, and adults in his church. He has drug rehab programs. He offers psychological counseling based on biblical principles. He's active in AIDS awareness programs, both here and in Africa. He's a man of action, and the action, as far as I can tell, is positive."

"So you're selling that fraud your church," says Mario.

"I didn't say that."

"You're implying as much, Albertina."

"You're jumping to conclusions, Mario."

"I see you jumping through that man's hoop."

"That's unfair."

"Sorry, Pastor, but I suppose men and women of the cloth have a natural affinity for one another."

I don't know what to say. Mario is being petulant. He keeps raising the stakes. I want to bring down the temperature, but I'm having a hard time doing so. On the drive home, he's still railing against Bishop, still accusing me of being a pawn. When I don't respond, he grows even angrier. When we reach my house he walks me to the door.

"I take your silence as a sign of hostility," he says.

"That's silly," I say. "I'm not saying anything because I don't want to escalate a silly argument."

"You can call me silly all day long, Pastor Merci, but what seems silly to you is dead serious to me. The church is a venal institution that has corrupted our community and intoxicated our people as powerfully as junk food, liquor, and drugs combined."

"Thank you for taking me to the play," I say, determined to avoid answering his charge.

"I'm sorry our friendship has to end on such a sour note," Mario says.

I'm shocked and saddened.

"Is that how you feel?"

"It is," he says bluntly. "Good night."

And with that, he's gone.

"My Man's Gone Now"

I love *Porgy and Bess.*

I know it has been criticized for showing black people in stereotypical ways. I know Sidney Poitier, who took on the role of Porgy in the movie version, had reservations about playing a man who had been emasculated. And I know some say the music pretends to be operatic but it's really not.

Well, I say the music is beautiful. The songs soar, and I love the score. Sitting in the great music hall in L.A. and hearing "Summertime" and "I Loves You, Porgy" and "I Got Plenty O' Nuttin' " is sheer joy. When Clifford Bloom said he had front-row tickets, I didn't hesitate. I never get tired of these melodies.

Clifford selects cultural events, usually music, he knows I'll like. He secures superb tickets. He dresses smartly and he seems to be able to sense whether I'm in a talkative mood or not. If I'm not, he'll keep the conversation to a minimum. If I am, he'll initiate a discussion on a topic sure to interest me.

After the performance, on the ride home, Clifford is playing a new release by Candi Staton. Like me, Candi sang the blues before becoming a Christian. Now she sings gospel and sings it beautifully. I love her. Her music comforts and inspires me. I make a mental note to call her and tell her how much I like her new record.

Clifford asks me if I know Candi. Again, it's as though he's reading my mind. When I tell him I do, he tells me that he knows Candi's producers. He tells me a few inside stories about the music business that I enjoy. Clifford has a way of keeping me amused.

When we reach my home, he walks me to the front door. It's a pleasant October evening, not too warm, not too cold. I have a couple of old rocking chairs on my front porch.

"Would you mind if we sat for a while and talked?" Clifford asked.

The weather is so nice I can't refuse.

"Not at all," I say.

We sit down. I see Clifford doesn't start rocking until he sees the rhythm of my rocking motion. I set the gentle tempo and he follows.

"We don't have much time before you have to make your decision," he says. "Just wondering if you'd like to talk about it."

He's right. The end of October is coming up.

"I'm delaying the decision until we have our big meeting on Wednesday."

"The consensus of that meeting, Albertina, is entirely in our hands."

"I can't be that sure, Clifford."

"I can. If you decide not to sell, I'll invite Ginger Johnson to the meeting and she'll arrive with a powerful half-hour visual presentation on why the historical integrity of the neighborhood will be ruined by the invasion of the megachurch. And even without Ginger's persuasive argument, the congregation is very much waiting to hear your point of view. You are much loved by your parishioners, Albertina, and we are quite prepared to back you in whatever you decide."

"So you think it's that simple, Clifford?"

"Yes, I do."

"I'll pray on it."

"Would you mind if I offered a short prayer, Albertina?"

"Of course not."

"Father God," Clifford prays, "direct our course, direct our thinking, open our minds to do what is right. Help us find ways to reflect and glorify You."

"Amen," I say, thinking that Clifford has concluded his prayer.

"And Father," he adds, reaching across his rocking chair and taking my hand, "I thank You for my blessings, and I especially thank You for my pastor, this wonderful woman whom I love with all my heart. In Jesus' name, Amen."

"I Can't Survive This"

"God's love allows us to survive anything," I tell my son.

"Not this. This is too much. It isn't just the pain of my wife leaving me, Mom. It's Nina leaving me four months after we got married. *Four months!* We haven't even sent out all the thank-you notes for our wedding presents. It's beyond humiliation, beyond shame. I can't tell anyone. I haven't even told Laura. I can't even admit it to myself. I keep thinking she's going to call and apologize and say she's on her way home. I keep hearing the key in the door and waiting for her to walk through."

"I'm sorry, son—"

"Maybe I made a mistake. Maybe I never should have told her that they weren't making my movie. When she found out that my screenplay was going up in smoke, that was it. Three days later she said she wasn't coming back from Hawaii. In my naïvely stupid way, I thought she'd console me. I thought Nina would help me through the crisis. Together, we'd find a way that I could handle the reality of what was happening—all my hopes and dreams dashed because a studio head changed his mind. But instead, my news convinced her I was the wrong guy for her. In her eyes, my future in Hollywood was ruined and I was ruined and she wanted nothing to do with me. I was a fool to tell her anything."

"No, you weren't, Andre, you were truthful. That's a good thing."

"There are no good things anymore for me. My life is over."

When her children go through a crisis, a mother's life stops. All other concerns seem small in comparison. The upcoming meeting at my church, the disagreement with Mario, my feelings about Clifford Bloom—all these matters go out the window. All that matters is that my son is hurting worse than he has ever hurt before. His pain becomes my pain. I desperately want to help. I want to do anything that will keep him from falling apart.

"It helps to talk, Andre. It will help if you tell me everything that you're feeling, knowing that I'm not judging you; I'm loving you as much as I ever have."

"It didn't help to talk to Dad."

"You told him?"

"Besides you, Mom, he's the only other person I've told. He said I should go after her. He said he'd send me money to get on a plane and fly to Maui and bring Nina back. He said I've been too lenient and too passive. He believes women want men who take charge. Dad says she's confused, and the only way to change that is if I end the confusion for her. But the truth, Mom, the truth is that if I show up in Hawaii that exercise guy would kick my butt. I've never had a fight in my life, and to march in there and demand that my wife return to me—well, I can't do it. I don't have the nerve. And the fact that I don't have the nerve fills me with even more self-disgust."

I want to tell my son that I feel his father's advice is ludicrous. Suddenly I feel a wave of anger and resentment washing over me. Ben Hunter is a fool when it comes to women. He's torturing his son with his ridiculous macho attitude. He doesn't know Nina and here he is urging Andre to act like a caveman and reclaim her. I want to tell Andre that his father is wrongheaded and ignorant. But no son wants to hear his father trashed. It's not my business to do so. That would only make matters worse. Besides, I don't need to impose my issues with Ben upon Andre. When divorced parents bad-mouth one another to their children, it's the children who suffer. I need to keep the focus on my son, not my former husband.

"God never views you with anything but love and acceptance," I tell Andre.

"I can't stand to be in my own company now, Mom. I feel like a completely weak and useless human being."

"We're all weak, son. The beautiful part is that our weakness allows us to lean on His strength."

"I can't hear any of that now, Mama. I really can't. Whatever His strength might be, I'm not feeling it. I'm not feeling anything but rage. But I don't even have the guts to act on that rage. That's how pathetic I am. I'm sorry, I can't talk about it anymore. . . ."

And with that, Andre hangs up.

I call back, but he doesn't answer.

I'm more than concerned. I'm a little frightened. I've never heard my son talk this way before. Since the start of his relationship with Nina, I've felt like he'd lost his emotional bearings. I've always said as much as I could say without overstepping my boundaries. But my suspicions were strong: I thought the woman had done a number on him. He was obsessed. He had lost his good sense. The woman was taking him for a ride.

Now it's clear that the ride isn't over yet. And my fear is that he'll wind up crashing. The combination is lethal: bad news over a screenplay he had worked on for nearly two years and the revelation of his wife's infidelity, all in the first few months of his marriage. With all my might, I try to find ways to pray for the person who inflicted this injury on my beloved son. I can't say I succeed. I can't say that my fury at Nina isn't overtaking my peace of mind.

How could she do this?

Has she no conscience?

I brush the questions aside and concentrate on Andre.
How can I help him?
Is it crazy for me to get on a plane and fly to New York?

I get on a plane and fly to New York. I leave early in the morning
and arrive at his apartment that evening. He is not unhappy to see
me. He looks terrible. He's in his bathrobe. It looks like he hasn't
slept or shaved in days. His eyes are red and swollen from crying.
"You didn't have to come here," he says.
"Yes, I did."
"Mama, there's nothing you can say. I don't want to hear about
Jesus and His saving grace. Not now. Words don't mean anything
to me. And no sermon can convince me otherwise."
"I'm not here to deliver a sermon," I say. "I'm here to take you
roller-skating."
"Roller-skating?"
"Yes, roller-skating. As a little boy, you made me take you to
the roller-skating rink. You could out–roller-skate anyone. You
were the best on our block. As a little girl, I wasn't half-bad my-
self. It's in your genes. So put on some clothes and let's go. I made
some calls and found a place in Brooklyn Heights."
"That's insane," he says.
"Maybe so, but I'm not taking no for an answer. So get dressed,
boy. We're going skating!"

A man in his thirties is still a boy. Maybe that's true of men in
their forties, fifties, and sixties. Who knows? As a woman in my
seventies, though, looking at my son sleeping on his sofa after
spending three hours roller-skating, I see him as a child. I remem-

ber those summers when he would play outside until the light of day disappeared and he'd finally come inside, exhausted and becalmed.

I think my suggestion that we go roller-skating was so bizarre that Andre, in his state of deep melancholy, was too shocked to resist. The inspiration came from out of the blue. Actually, I believe it came from the Lord because I asked the Lord for direction. On the plane to New York, I was fresh out of ideas. How do I comfort Andre? How do I help him through this crisis? What words will work? What Scriptures, what advice? Nothing came to mind. And then in the cab from the airport to his apartment, one word did it: skating.

He sleeps that evening until midnight. When he awakens, I fix him a bowl of soup, and after eating he goes back to sleep. He sleeps till noon the next day.

"I can't remember the last time I've slept so late," he says.

"You were exhausted," I tell him. "You needed the rest."

I cook him a big breakfast that he wolfs down in no time. I make us a pot of coffee. After a second cup, he starts talking.

"I'm working on a new screenplay," says Andre. "I need to get back to it."

"You will. You love to write, son. Writing is your gift."

"I miss her."

"I'm sure you do."

"And I love her. You don't doubt that, Mom, do you?"

"No, I don't."

"I try to hate her and I can't."

"You have a good heart, Andre, an understanding heart."

"But this humiliation. This humiliation is heavier than anything I've ever faced. When do I start telling people what happened? And who do I tell?"

"I'm going to talk about the God we worship," I say.

"Go ahead, Mama."

"The God we worship suffered humiliation of the most extreme kind. You know the story as well as I do. He suffered shame. He suffered abandonment and betrayal. He was made the object of scorn and public ridicule. The God we worship went through it all. He went through it for us. Jesus went through it not only to save us but to show us that His love will overwhelm the worst humiliation. His love will overwhelm all ridicule, scorn, and shame. He told us to give Him our burdens and our pains. They're too heavy for you, He said, but nothing's too heavy for Me. He said, Let your weakness make you strong in your faith in Me. Do you believe Him, son?"

"I do."

"Then take Him at His word, Andre. Lay your burdens at His feet. Let Him set you free."

The Big Meeting

My head is spinning from that whirlwind three-day trip to New York. My mind is still on Andre. We talk every night and I continue to encourage him to move forward with his life.

Several times a day I pray to understand God's will for my church. The prayer is short and silent.

"It's not about me, Lord. It's about You."

I haven't heard from Mr. Mario and must say that I miss his company. But there's no time to worry about that. Clifford Bloom has been my rock of support for this upcoming showdown. He offers me constant and strong sympathy.

"I know you've been praying, Albertina," he says. "And I know you want to do what is right before God."

"I know this church must be saved," I say.

He assures me that Naomi Cohen's cousin Ginger will be there for the meeting with a whole team of West Adams District historical preservationists to argue the case against demolishing our building.

"When the congregation hears her arguments," says Clifford, "they will overwhelmingly vote in your favor."

Without my telling him, Clifford understands that my position is to keep our beloved building intact. He knows that, despite all the pressure to tear it down, I have to save it. It means so much to me. And besides, it is a jewel, a pristine piece of architecture now dedicated to the glory of God. In the face of Bishop Gold's claims about the good the new megachurch will do, I have to stand my ground and preserve a church I feel is right and true. Besides, there's lots of land all over Los Angeles County. With their millions, Fellowship of Faith can find another parcel just as big. If their work is good, God will see to it that it gets done.

Justine and I go to get our hair done on the morning of the Big Meeting. We both patronize Blondie's Salon on Crenshaw Boulevard where I've gone for years. Blondie has been my loyal hairdresser since I was singing the blues. She's a wonderful woman who has traveled with everyone from Gladys to Aretha. Blondie understands style. She knows I'm conservative, but she also knows I like a little flair.

"How about a little flip in front, Tina?" she asks. "It'll be bold, but not too bold. Seems like tonight you may need to be a little bold."

Justine is sitting next to me talking about how Clarence Withers has been delivering her mail nearly every evening. Now he wants to take her to Bermuda.

"Justine, what does your friend from Target think about all this?"

"Johnny Marbee? They sent Johnny out to New York to give him special managerial training. He'll be gone for nearly a month."

I don't say a word.

"I hear what you're thinking," says Justine.

"I'm thinking about tonight."

"I'll be with you tonight, Tina. All your friends will be there. You don't have a thing to worry about."

Justine's not a regular church member, but this fight with Fellowship of Faith has her worked up. She has actually been showing up on Sundays recently.

"Something about that Bishop I don't like and don't trust," Justine says. "I grew up with jive-turkey preachers, and I can smell 'em a mile away. I know you're not about to give in to him, are you?"

"Well, it's not just me who has the final say-so, it's the congregation."

"I don't see them going against their pastor, do you?"

"I want to hear them out," I say. "It's important that they have their say. I need to be open about this whole thing."

"I know you, Albertina Merci. Bishop may be a slick old dog, but you got the man's number. He ain't pulling no fast one on my girl Tina."

"Thank you for your vote of confidence," I say as I inspect the way that Blondie has given my hair a flip. It suits me well. I feel ready to for this long-awaited confrontation.

House of Trust is filled beyond capacity. Even the folding chairs set up in the aisles can't hold the crowd. The atmosphere is electric. I can feel the buzz. I can hear it. Everyone is chattering. My nephew Patrick is looking dashing in a midnight blue Italian-cut suit. He comes over and kisses me.

"Great to you see, Aunt Albertina," he says.

"God bless you, Patrick," I say. "You look terrific." I see Rabbi Naomi Cohen looking at me and Patrick. I smile and wave. She's with her friend Roger Stein, the public radio producer.

Naomi's cousin Ginger Johnson comes over and says, "On Clifford's suggestion, I've prepared a comprehensive ten-minute presentation to explain the historical necessity of maintaining this church. I've brought four other experts in my field to back me up."

"That's wonderful, Ginger," I say. "The members of the church will be interested in everything you have to say."

As I take my place before the podium, I see Bishop Gold and his son Solomon enter the sanctuary. They smile and acknowledge me politely. Accompanying them are two distinguished-looking African American gentlemen wearing pin-striped suits. They both carry large briefcases.

I begin with a prayer. "Let's stand," I say, "and hold our neighbor's hand. Father God, help us tonight to listen to one another with open hearts and open minds. Let us pray for the person standing to our right. Let us pray for the person standing to our left. May he or she be relieved of all burdens. May our spirit of friendship and generosity move our neighbor to move closer to You. Let us pray for each other. Let us leave self-concern behind. Let us forget our prejudices and our preconceptions. Let Your spirit guide us, Oh Lord, and let Your spirit open our eyes to clarity. Let us grow in wisdom and grow in gratitude for the wonders of this new life You have given us in Christ Jesus, Amen.

"I know many people want to speak tonight, and everyone will have their turn. As I explained in our church bulletin, we will first conduct this open meeting and then excuse all nonmembers so the parishioners of House of Trust can speak among ourselves and come to a consensus. With that in mind, I'd like to invite Bishop Gold to speak first."

"Thank you, Pastor," says Bishop, standing up at once. "Your courtesy and spirit of Christian love are a joy, not only for those blessed to be a part of your marvelous congregation, but also for those of us who have come to know you as a friend and fellow disciple of Christ. Rather than dominate this meeting with our point of view, though, we would much rather listen to those with other points of view first. As your moving prayer so eloquently urged, our desire is to open our minds and our hearts to the positions of others."

"Thank you, Bishop," I say. I don't entirely trust his words. I feel that this man always has his own agenda, but who am I to judge? Maybe he's had a change of heart and really is willing to listen. At the same time, who are those gentlemen sitting next to him carrying those ominous attaché cases? Why are they here?

"Very well," I continue. "If there are no objections, then, let's begin with Ginger Johnson, a recognized expert in the field of urban preservation. She has studied the history of this neighborhood for several years at the University of California School of Urban Planning. Ms. Johnson and her colleagues have prepared an overview of our situation."

Ginger is brilliant. She's a clear and succinct speaker and breaks down the case both verbally and pictorially. She gives a history of the bank before we turned it into House of Trust, and shows several stunning vintage photos. She compares those photos with our restoration, emphasizing the accuracy and continuity between the old and the new. We saved the fixtures; we saved the woodwork; we saved the exterior façade; we integrated the original plan and modified only what we had to.

"House of Trust," says Ginger, "is a model of loving care and respect for what was here. And what was here was not only good, but splendid, a building constructed during an age when European materials and construction techniques were utilized. European artisans were brought in to do the actual work. The work represents an era in the history of this city that is, at once, glorious and fascinating. Even more important, this building is our living history. To destroy that history is to destroy part of ourselves. How foolish would that be! How irresponsible! This congregation should be lauded for the loving care it has extended to the architectural legacy of Los Angeles. To turn around and betray that legacy—to turn this magnificent marble into a pile of rubble— would be a crime. I beseech each of you in the name of all that is right and reasonable: Do not commit such a crime. You have done something beautiful and good in restoring this noble building. By turning it into the House of Trust, you have inspired this city to trust you, to look to you for leadership. This building carries a spirit that must not be destroyed. It is a spirit that nourishes us all."

The audience rises to their feet and gives Ginger a rousing reception. The applause goes on for several minutes. I cannot be more pleased. I can see in my congregants' eyes that she has convinced them. And as if that weren't enough, two of her colleagues follow up with short presentations of their own, reemphasizing what Ginger has said about the uniqueness of our building and the necessity of keeping it intact. Things couldn't be going better.

I see Naomi Cohen and Roger Stein smiling broadly. Clifford Bloom winks at me knowingly. My nephew Patrick, seated with Solomon and Bishop, looks uncomfortable. I look around and fail to see Mr. Mario, but that should be no surprise. He has yet to step foot inside this church.

I ask if there are others who wish to speak on behalf of the current church location. No hands are raised; apparently Ginger and the others have made their point.

"Bishop Gold," I say. "If you'd be kind enough to address us at this time, we'd be grateful."

"I'm the one who's filled with gratitude, Pastor," he says as he makes his way to the front of the sanctuary. "I'm grateful to be able to address this thoughtful and intelligent gathering of people. And grateful to be able to say that we are all in agreement. My own people did similar research and our conclusions match Ms. Johnson's. We've concluded, in short, that our original intention, to tear down this church to clear the way for a Fellowship of Faith megaconstruction, was shortsighted and, if you will, architecturally and historically irresponsible."

I'm shocked. So is the congregation. Is Bishop caving in? Have I won this battle outright? Has a confrontation been avoided?

"Yes," he says in his mellifluous manner. "It's wonderful when the saints are in agreement. We can praise God for harmony, praise Him when like-minded and God-fearing people see potential conflict and find a way to overcome strife. There is no conflict here. There is no strife. There is only conviction on the part of Fellowship of Faith that House of Trust must be kept intact, as is, a precious artifact of a past age. That's why our original plan has been shredded and, in its place, an entirely new plan conceived. Gentlemen . . . if you will . . ."

Bishop points to the two men who are seated in the same row as Solomon and Patrick. The briefcases in tow, they join Bishop at the front of the sanctuary.

"May I introduce Deacons Frank and Duncan Hoxie. In addition to being long-term deacons in the Fellowship of Faith in Dallas, these brothers are distinguished members of the American Institute of Architects. Their designs for the United Insurance Company skyscraper in Atlanta and the headquarters for Mutual Steel in Birmingham have won international prizes—not to mention their museum for African American history recently built in New York. Frank and Duncan are far more qualified to discuss our new plan than I am. They are, after all, its architects, so, if you would allow me to turn the program over to them, I would be grateful."

Duncan does the speaking as Frank takes out a laptop computer set up for a PowerPoint presentation. A large viewing screen is placed against the wall and within seconds we're looking at a startling composite image: The House of Trust is shown as is— the same façade, the same building—only now it is surrounded on both sides and on top by an enormous construction two hundred yards long and three stories tall.

"Indeed," says Duncan Hoxie, "we are committed to saving this building. We are committed to not changing one iota of this brilliant restoration. We agree with Ms. Johnson when she said it would be a crime to do so. We have instead found a way to build around it, to build to its left and to its right, to build above it while keeping this precious jewel intact. As you can see from our renderings, we have altered the façade of our new Fellowship of

Faith to reflect the original 1920s style with its lovely oversized windows and bas-reliefs of birds and flowers. The new style will mimic the original, not the other way around. Nothing about House of Trust will be changed. The church and its building will be, in fact, celebrated, perfectly preserved and framed in a manner guaranteed to bring out its warm character and unique charm."

I'm speechless, but the church members aren't. They seem impressed by what Bishop and the Hoxie brothers have rendered. Member after member gets up to say how ingenious they find the plan, how they appreciate the lengths to which Fellowship of Faith has gone to consider our position and modify it accordingly. One member wants to know how could I possibly object?

Ginger Johnson answers for me. She finds words before I do. I'm still too shocked to react.

"This is a sacrilege," Ginger says. "You're taking a delicate and small building and constructing a monster around it. If you do this, the very character of the House of Trust, sitting inside this monolith, will be destroyed, its sense of autonomy gone forever. Your solution is not a solution. Your solution is an atrocity. You're co-opting rather than cooperating; you're committing an architectural crime of the first degree. Gentlemen, whatever your intentions, you have made matters worse."

When Ginger is through speaking, her colleagues, Rabbi Cohen, Roger Stein, Justine, and Clifford Bloom, all rise to applaud. They are alone. No one else is clapping.

The Hoxie brothers vigorously defend their plan, giving examples of other cities where old buildings have become the cornerstones of new ones without losing their authenticity. Bishop Gold talks about how Fellowship of Faith would revitalize our neighborhood. He recites a litany of statistics, each more impressive than the next: lower crime, higher employment, more after-school programs for kids, sports, arts, Christian lectures and Christian plays. "Plus," he adds, "Pastor Merci and House of Trust will be left entirely alone to conduct your spiritual affairs any way you see fit. If at some point you chose to join Fellowship of Faith we would be honored and will do whatever we can to make that transition smooth and beneficial for the pastor and members of House of Trust. But that decision is entirely yours, not ours. You will remain an independent church."

I'm still too overwhelmed to respond. Instead, I ask Bishop and the architects whether they have any more to add.

"Of course construction can be loud and inconvenient," says Duncan Hoxie, "but you have our word that no work will be done on weekends. In spite of the expense, we're committed to do the heaviest construction late at night. We do not want to disturb the daytime activities at House of Trust."

When the presentation is finally complete, I ask all nonmembers to leave. They file out silently.

"Saints," I say, "I'm interested in your reaction to this new plan. Please come up and share your point of view."

Clifford Bloom is first.

"I don't like it," he says. "They're surrounding us. They're encapsulating us. They're putting us in a box. I don't want that megachurch sitting on top of my head and squeezing me on all sides. I think the plan is crazy."

"I think the plan is good," says Grace Brown, a longtime member who began worshiping with me when I was preaching at home. "They've gone out of their way to save our building. What else can they do? I think these people respect us, and I think they'll help our neighborhood. We couldn't ask for more understanding and more flexible partners. Besides, having a Christian movie theater and a gym and a theater for spiritual plays, all right down the street—who can object to that?"

No one. No one except Clifford Bloom objects.

"All right," I say with a heavy heart, "it seems clear we have a consensus."

The Blues Ain't Nothing
But a Pain in Your Heart

The blues are part of life. Always have been. Always will be. I love the Lord and pray to Him every day, but I never expect that the blues will disappear forever. Everyone gets the blues. But prayer makes me mindful that the blues are a sometime thing, the blues come and go, and by invoking God's grace and His ever-flowing love, I can shorten the time I spend with the blues. But I can't eliminate them. Not entirely.

Today I got the blues. There's a song that says, "Today I Sing the Blues." Well, baby, I'm singing them. Albertina got snookered. Albertina got taken. Albertina got outsmarted and outmaneuvered. Albertina was playing outside her league. Albertina got whupped something fierce.

First Kings 4:29 says, "God gave Solomon wisdom and very great discernment and breadth of mind, like the sand that is on the seashore." That makes me think that the best thing I can do today, rather than follow my routine by going to my church office at seven a.m., is to head for the beach instead. I need to take a walk and clear my head. I always mean to walk the beach, but somehow I never get around to it. The demands of the day distract me from that pleasure. Today, though, it seems more a necessity than a pleasure. I need quiet reflection. I need to seek the wisdom that allowed Solomon to make wise and righteous decisions.

On the drive to Santa Monica, I stay focused on the changing light, the break of day, the dark gray of the sky turning pale blue. The transformation is a daily miracle. I seek such a transformation for myself. My heart is dark gray. My heart is anguished. The thought of being boxed in by Bishop Gold's megachurch is deeply depressing. It will mean that House of Trust cannot escape the culture that comes with a corporate-style church. I am not against such churches. Obviously people love them or these churches wouldn't experience such growth. I do not stand in judgment of other Christian institutions. At the same time, I feel that God has directed me to lead House of Trust with simplicity. We don't want to form a committee in charge of forming other committees.

Or do we?

I reach the beach and park my car. The ocean is calm today. The waves break quietly. Seagulls flutter along the shore. I take off my shoes and walk along the water's edge. The sand is cool and refreshes the bottom of my feet. The noise inside my head is still loud. *Why was my congregation so completely taken in by Bishop's plan? Why don't they realize that we're being compromised? What can I do to convince them? Is it my job to convince them? Maybe they're right and I'm wrong.*

The ocean is so vast, so beautiful, so peaceful. I pray that peace of mind will wash over me.

"God," I pray out loud, "allow me to accept whatever conditions arise. Grant me the serenity to see clearly. Cleanse me of oppositional anger and vindictive drive. Your will, Oh Lord, let me do Your will."

I walk for a good hour, just concentrating on the sea, the sky, the ever-changing light. The sun breaks through a curtain of haze. A sandpiper scurries by. An older man braves the cold water, diving into the face of a wave.

Acceptance, acceptance, acceptance.

When I get back home, there are many calls on my answering machine, but the first two are from Mr. Mario and Clifford Bloom.

"It's Sad"

Those were the only words on Mr. Mario's message. I found them confusing and, to be honest, infuriating.

What's sad?

I knew he was provoking me to call him back, and I did; I wanted to know what he considered so sad.

"The fact," he said, "that you have capitulated."

"Who says I have?"

"Two friends were at the meeting and told me after you heard Bishop's outrageous proposal to build on top of your church, you agreed."

"I didn't agree. I listened to my members respond—that's all I did."

"And they loved the idea."

"They seemed to, yes."

"And that's enough for you to capitulate?"

"That's enough for me to give weighty consideration to the wishes of those I serve."

"It's sad."

"You already said that."

"You're not only allowing your church to be co-opted by a megachurch; you're actually going to be swallowed whole by the leviathan. You'll never get out."

"Jonah got out of the whale, didn't he?"

"You still live by fairy tales."

"I live by faith."

"Albertina, I'm just trying to help you."

"By berating me?"

"By making you see what happened to you."

"As if I don't know," I say.

"You don't want to admit that your Christian brother is dishon-est, crass, and manipulative. You don't want to see how deeply corrupt the church has become. Or, better yet, how corrupt the church has always been."

"If, by 'the church,'" I say, "you mean the teachings and exam-ple of the church, then those are incorruptible. God is pure. We fall short of His lessons, and for that we are forgiven."

"So you're telling me that you've forgiven Bishop."

"He has his agenda for spreading the Word. I have mine."

"Then you're willing to live with the situation."

"I didn't say that."

"Then what are you saying?"

"I'm saying good-bye, Mario. Thank you for calling but I have work to do."

"I think I can work on the membership," says Clifford Bloom when I return his call.

"I appreciate your support, Clifford," I say, "but maybe we should wait a while."

"Then it might be too late."

"I know you want to help. Right now, though, I just need to pray."

"I'm there for you, Albertina," says Clifford. "Whenever and whatever you need, count on me. I'm devoted."

"I know you are."

"My devotion is based on more than friendship," he adds. "It's based on love."

Those aren't words I want to hear right now, but at the same time I don't want to be short-tempered or cruel.

"All acts of kindness are based on God's love," I say.

There is silence. The silence becomes awkward.

"Will you call me when you need me?" he asks.

"I will, Clifford, and I want you to know how much I value your concern."

There are times, I think to myself when I get off the phone, *when people can be too concerned. People can crowd you. Well-intentioned friends can try to rescue you when you aren't sure whether you need rescuing. Men can express their love at the wrong time. Or maybe I'm just cranky. Or confused. Maybe I don't want to talk—or be talked to—at this time.*

When the phone rings next, I look at the caller ID and see RABBI NAOMI COHEN. I pick up the receiver.

"I'm so sorry, Albertina," says Naomi. "Last night must have been devastating for you."

"It took me by surprise, baby."

"You probably need a little more time to process everything that happened," Naomi continues, "but I just want you to know that my cousin Ginger is prepared to go on the offensive. She's readying an extensive public relations campaign to galvanize the neighborhood against Bishop's hideous new supersanctuary. My friend Roger Stein also wants to help. He was horrified by the proposal. He wants to do a feature on public radio and tell the whole story. Would you be willing to be interviewed?"

"Right now, dear, I have my congregation to consider. They liked the idea. They liked Bishop Gold's proposal. And I can understand why. I'm trying to see it from their perspective, Naomi, because their perspective is important. I don't want to start a war between myself and my parishioners, especially if the issue isn't about anything more than a physical building."

"Pardon me for saying so, Pastor, but it is about more than that, isn't it? Isn't it about encroachment and a clash of values? Isn't it about the culture of one church dominating another?"

I don't answer.

"Baby," I finally say, "at this point I'm not sure what it's about. But I know you mean well and act out of love."

"Despite what happened with Patrick," says Naomi, "our congregation feels extremely close to yours. When I told my members what happened, they were visibly upset. They love House of Trust."

I don't know what to say. I'm feeling emotional, even on the verge of tears.

"We'll talk about this soon, sweetheart," I say. "Let me call you later in the week."

Later in the week my nephew Patrick calls to say, "Bishop Gold, Solomon, and I would like to contribute to next month's Thanksgiving program, Aunt Albertina. We'd like to donate two hundred meals. Twenty of our members have volunteered to help you."

"That's kind of you, Patrick," I say.

"I hope you're feeling okay about our construction project," he adds.

"How do you feel about it?" I ask.

He pauses before answering, "I believe it's inevitable."

The Spare Bedroom

I don't know the literal meaning of a nervous breakdown. We use the term loosely, and when I hear it applied to someone, I usually think that person simply can't cope.

When my son, Andre, uses those words to describe his condition, my response is to question him gently about what's going on.

He just keeps repeating the words, as though he's haunted: "I'm breaking down, Mama. I'm breaking down . . ."

He doesn't want to hear about skating or any other diversion. He isn't working, isn't eating, isn't reaching out to his friends.

"Are you praying, Andre?" I ask him.

"No."

"Can we pray together now on the phone?"

"Not really in the mood, Mom."

"Would you like to come home for a while?"

"Maybe."

"You were coming home for Thanksgiving to be with me and Laura anyway. Now you'll get here just a little bit sooner. That will give you something to look forward to, baby, won't it?"

"There's really nothing to look forward to," he says. "Nothing really matters."

We hang up and I pray, *"Father, guide my son. Let him feel Your love, Your mercy, Your grace. Let him be led by Your light."*

Later that day I decide to call my friend Florence Ginzburg, a clinical psychologist. Florence and I graduated high school together and have remained close ever since. She invites me over to her apartment in the Fairfax District for a cup of tea.

In confidence, I tell her what Andre has been going through. Florence is a wise and compassionate listener. You can feel her soul when she speaks.

"Taking him skating, Albertina, was a wonderful idea," she says. "Encouraging action is extremely helpful."

"But now he says there's nothing he wants to do."

"Yet he's coming home to you," says Florence. "That's action."

"But is that enough?" I ask.

"You know, Albertina, I have to admit something to you, but I'm a little embarrassed."

"Please, Florence, say whatever's on your mind."

"I had a patient last weekend whose story parallels Andre's. She's a young woman who has suffered painful rejection, from both her work and her boyfriend. She's distraught and practically nonfunctional. Because she has a Christian background, I thought of asking your advice. You see, Albertina, it has taken me some years to realize this, but now I believe we're basically in the same business. We're trying to restore people's souls. And in that area, your instincts and expertise far outweigh mine."

"You're kind to say so, Florence."

"I don't say it out of kindness, dear, but deep respect. I've watched you closely. I've seen you minister to people's needs. And even though I don't for a minute doubt the wisdom of psychology books or the benefits of therapy, I also believe that the deepest healing must come in the spiritual realm. That's why I'll be so interested to see how you meet this challenge. And meet it you will. You'll meet it because it's love that leads your actions."

"What you call love," I say, "I call Jesus."

"I value our friendship, Albertina, and I'd be deeply grateful if you let me know how the God you call Jesus resolves this crisis with Andre."

First Peter 4:12–13 says: "Beloved, do not be surprised at the fiery ordeal among you, which comes upon you for your testing, as though some strange thing were happening to you; but to the degree that you share the sufferings of Christ, keep on rejoicing, so that also at the revelation of His glory you may rejoice with exultation."

I'm home alone, standing in the spare bedroom where Andre will be staying, when I read this passage out loud.

I read it again, my voice growing louder: *Beloved, do not be surprised at the fiery ordeal among you, which comes upon you for your testing, as though some strange thing were happening to you; but to the degree that you share the sufferings of Christ, keep on rejoicing, so that also at the revelation of His glory you may rejoice with exultation.*

A son suffers.

A mother suffers when she learns her child is in pain.

It's a fiery ordeal. It's a testing. It's some strange thing. But the amazing thing is that God's Word says that we're sharing the suffering with His Son. And in doing so, we can keep on rejoicing.

At the moment of understanding, at the moment of revelation, joy enters my heart. I can't explain it. I can't understand it. But the Bible gives me clarity; the Bible gives me hope. The Word of God *is* hope.

I change the sheets on the bed and retire for the night.

I sleep in peace.

The Pains of Childbirth

Come Sunday I'm in the pulpit at House of Trust. My mind is on my children. A woman can have many roles, but motherhood is always first. Motherhood is deep. And deep in my thoughts are my son Darryl, and the way he died, and my daughter, Laura, and her struggles as a schoolteacher, and my son Andre, who says he is breaking down. I think of each of their births. Each time labor was long and difficult. But the labor was joyful.

I read Romans 8:22 to my congregation: "For we know that the whole creation groans and suffers the pains of childbirth together until now."

"What's the meaning?" I ask. "The meaning is that the new Adam has birthed us into a life entirely new, entirely glorious, entirely free. We can accept the gift of our rebirth, we can embrace the victory over the cross, we can celebrate the resurrection every day and every way."

After the service, many of the parishioners come up to me and express surprise that I didn't address the issue of Fellowship of Faith's building plan. They want to hear that I'm as excited about the plan as they are. With few exceptions, they're eager for my endorsement.

"I'm glad Bishop convinced you along with the rest of us," presumes Kathleen Underwood, a CPA and one of my most faithful parishioners.

"To be honest," I say, "I still have reservations."

"Well, then why didn't you express them at the meeting, Pastor?"

"Wanted to reflect a little longer. I don't like being hasty in judgments."

"But on reflection," says Kathleen, "you understand how much this could mean for our community, don't you?"

"I understand that most of the House of Trust members have their hearts set on seeing Fellowship of Faith move on the block."

"Not only move on the block," adds Kathleen, "but add to our prestige as a church. Plus, they're eager to partner with us in so many good ways. I see it as having the best of both worlds."

"I understand what you're saying, Kathleen."

"And you agree?"

"I agree, Kathleen dear, that the body of Christ needs to be unified and not divided by self-interest. I'll do anything to work for that unification."

"That's why we love you, Pastor."

"I love you too, sweetheart."

Clifford Bloom invites me to dinner and a concert at a place called the Jazz Bakery. I accept, mainly because I want to see the artist who is performing: Little Jimmy Scott. I've known Jimmy ever since Ray Charles produced him in the early sixties.

Clifford and I eat in a little bistro in Culver City, close to the venue. I'm not in a talkative mood, and Clifford's sensitivity picks up on that. He senses that I am in deep deliberation about how to handle the battle that has been so brilliantly planned by Bishop Gold. Clifford has told me before that he's willing to fight them off with me, but since I am not bringing up the subject, Clifford wisely leaves it alone.

That's why Clifford is wonderful. He knows me so well. He knows when to leave me alone and when to invite me to hear soothing music. No music is more soothing to me than Little Jimmy Scott's haunting voice. He is a small man whose voice is high and filled with pain. He sings of his life, of having lost his mother when he was a child. He sings "Sometimes I Feel Like a Motherless Child." He sings of nights of loneliness, of wanting "Someone to Watch over Me." When he sings, I not only feel the sweetness of his soul, I feel the strength of his conviction. I feel him crying out for God. His songs may be secular, but they are prayers, and his prayers are sincere. I believe every note he sings. His singing helps heal my wounded heart.

"Thank you, Clifford," I say after Little Jimmy's performance.

"I was sure that would help you."

"You were right," I add.

Afterward, on the way home, Clifford doesn't analyze what he heard or show off his knowledge of Little Jimmy's music. In the past, Clifford would have done that. But the more we've gone out, the more he's learned to read me right. The fact that he has bothered to study me is a lesson in kindness and patience.

When we get to my house, he walks me to the door and sees me safely inside. He knows I want to be alone for now and gets me to promise that I'll call him if I need anything, anything at all.

Church of the Nazarene

"Patrick, I'm glad you called me," I tell my nephew. "I was just about to call you. Are you in L.A.?"

"I'm in Dallas, Aunt Albertina."

"Well, I hope you'll be here for Thanksgiving, baby."

"I'll be there, and thanks for asking. In fact, I was just calling you to get Andre's number in New York. I've been wanting to talk to him."

"Well, I'm sure he'd love to hear from you."

"I have this idea, Aunt Albertina. When the Fellowship of Faith opens in L.A., we want to start a writing program. So many of our young people are interested in screenwriting, and I thought that Andre, if he were inclined to spend some time back home, might be willing to do some teaching. He'd be perfect for the job."

I think: *Still another reason to allow the building project to go through. But perhaps it's something to help get Andre back on his feet.*

Is this a signal that it's time for me to soften my position and give in to what Patrick says is inevitable?

"Talk to him by all means, Patrick," I say, without revealing any of Andre's current difficulties. If Andre wants to confide in Patrick, that's his choice, not mine. The two boys have always gotten along splendidly. Andre was furious with Patrick for quitting House of Trust, but maybe his anger has softened. Maybe Patrick's idea is a Godsend.

I give him Andre's number and say, "God bless you, Patrick."

"God bless you, Aunt Albertina. Thank you for finally understanding."

Understanding *what?*

I don't ask.

I don't want to know.

I just want to go on with my Thanksgiving day plan.

Thanksgiving arrives.

Our church kitchen serves hundreds of hot meals, with the help of volunteers from Fellowship of Faith. They are highly organized and efficient, far more so than we are. In fact, their plans are so well worked out in advance that I find myself taking a backseat. I'm usually in charge, but not this time. Which feels strange. But when I see how many more people are being fed, how can I object? If I'm learning to be less in control, maybe that's a good thing. If—or when—Fellowship of Faith surrounds House of Trust on all sides, my role will surely be reduced. I will no longer be needed the way I am needed now. Maybe that's the message my congregation is sending me.

I leave the church kitchen at about six. I've been there since seven that morning, but there's little for me to do now. Fellowship of Faith has it under control. Their workers come and go in shifts. Meals will be handed out till midnight. I must go home to my guests and serve Thanksgiving dinner.

Since Andre arrived, he and Patrick have been together virtually every minute. At first, Andre was still upset with Patrick for joining Fellowship of Faith, but apparently Patrick has explained his reasons persuasively. When I arrive home, they're talking in the living room.

"We'll get out tomorrow night and go to a gospel concert," says Patrick. "Kirk Franklin is performing. I remember that you're a Kirk Franklin fan."

"You remember right," says Andre.

"That settles it then. We'll make an evening of it."

Patrick seems to be an energizing influence on Andre. Thank God.

Within minutes, the others arrive. Laura is here from Chicago. Clifford Bloom comes through the door with a big bouquet of flowers and a box set of Sarah Vaughan CDs. Justine is accompanied by Clarence Withers, her friend from the post office. Her Target friend has been transferred to Minneapolis, thus uncomplicating her normally complicated love life.

"Pastor!" exclaims Marianne David, my new friend from Dallas, "your house is adorable!"

Marianne is here with her husband, Norman, her babies—three-year-old Esther and eleven-month-old Elizabeth—and her mom, Maureen, whose recovery from heart surgery has been remarkable.

We sit down to the table and pray.

"Father God," I say, "how You bless us! How You love us! How miraculously You bring us together when we need to be together! How You make our life an adventure of discovery and joy! We pray for those in need, for all those lost and looking for the healing love that You provide. In the name of Jesus, we say Amen."

The evening is lovely. Clifford and Clarence talk about jazz. Justine and Laura discuss Beyoncé's latest look.

Maureen is tending to her granddaughters when Norm and Marianne ask if they can speak with me privately.

"Of course, children," I say, "let's talk in the kitchen while I start cleaning up."

"I'll help," offers Marianne.

"Pastor," says Norm, who's also assisting me with the dishes, "I have something for you."

He hands me an envelope.

"For heaven's sake," I say, "I hope this isn't a gift. You didn't have to give me anything."

"It's not a gift," says Norm, "it's a plane ticket."

"Plane ticket?"

"For Dallas. I wish it were first-class, but our church doesn't have that kind of money."

"Your church?"

"The Church of the Nazarene," he explains. "Your mother's church."

"I don't understand," I admit.

"Our pastor is leaving after Christmas, and we've been searching for another. And when Marianne and I mentioned you, and told them your background, well, the whole congregation got excited and chipped in to buy a ticket. They're dying to meet you. Would you consider it, Pastor?"

I don't know what to say.

Hip-Hop Scholar

The lecture has begun.

Clifford and I are in the auditorium of the downtown Los Angeles Public Library. The crowd is excited because Dr. Cornel West of Princeton University is at the lectern. Behind him are a rapper and a deejay, who is manipulating two turntables. Dr. West is speaking of Dr. Martin King and the legacy of nonviolence. When West pauses, the rapper fills in the silence with rhymes about fallen leaders. When the rapper pauses, the deejay scratches old-school soul music grooves from the sixties. It's an exciting presentation.

With his woolly Afro and fuzzy beard, Dr. West lectures in the cadences of a Baptist preacher. His ideas, like the rapper's, come at the audience in great bursts of energy. I'm completely enthralled by West's idiosyncratic method of teaching.

Then something shifts for me: In the middle of the performance, I see Mr. Mario walking down the aisle with a woman on his arm. They find seats a few rows in front of us. I recognize his companion as City Councilwoman Rita Richardson, an attractive African American woman in her late fifties.

It's difficult for me to concentrate on the rest of the lecture. My thoughts are scattered. I have to admit to strong feelings of jealousy.

Fortunately, eventually the combination of Dr. West, the rapper, and the deejay is compelling enough to draw me back into the substance of the lecture. When it's over, Dr. West invites questions from the floor. Mr. Mario is the first to raise his hand. He stands as he starts to speak.

"With this new memorial in Washington, D.C.," says Mario, "don't we run the risk of sanitizing Dr. King's message? Don't we run the risk of rendering him harmless when, in fact, the thrust of this work was to challenge the status quo?"

Dr. West recognizes Mario from his theatrical roles and calls him by name. "My dear brother Mario," says West, "I think that risk surely does exist. If we turn Dr. King into a black Santa Claus, we will have, in fact, dishonored his legacy."

The men continue their dialogue much to the delight of the audience. Their banter is scintillating, and when Mr. Mario sits down he's given a rousing round of applause.

After the lecture is over, Clifford Bloom stops to speak to some acquaintances. Mr. Mario and Councilwoman Richardson approach the stage to engage Dr. West in further discussion. When Clifford and I are leaving, Mario still hasn't spotted me. I'm relieved.

Across the street in the Daily Grill restaurant, Clifford and I find a quiet booth in the back and order dinner.

"Mario Pani certainly is a brilliant man," says Clifford. "I'm glad he's looking so fit."

I change the subject and comment on Dr. West's unusual approach to the subject matter. But before I can complete my thought, I see Mario and Councilwoman Richardson heading in our direction. There's no avoiding them.

"Albertina," says Mario, "were you at Dr. West's lecture?"

"I was," I say, before introducing Mario to Clifford. I've known Councilwoman Richardson for years.

Mario is familiar with Clifford from Clifford's radio work.

"Please join us," Clifford urges Mario and Ms. Richardson.

"We wouldn't want to disturb you," says Mario.

"No disturbance at all," counters Clifford.

Ms. Richardson sits next to Clifford as Mr. Mario slips into the booth next to me. I'm extremely uncomfortable.

In contrast, Clifford is extremely comfortable. He peppers Mario with questions about his career and Mario cheerfully answers them all. Clifford asks Mario how he knows me.

"We're old friends," says Mario. "Dear friends."

Ms. Richardson knows about the church controversy and asks me how it will be resolved.

"With patience," I assure her. "Right now, though, things are still up in the air."

Mario peppers Clifford with questions about jazz, and the two men have a fine time exchanging views. From all outward appearances, it looks like we're having a grand time. Except for me, everyone is talkative.

The men argue over the check. Clifford wins the argument.

"We should double-date again," says Mr. Mario.

"Wonderful idea," Clifford agrees.

I don't say a word.

Museum of Tolerance

"This building has a holy aura about it," I say. "It feels sacred."

"It is sacred," Rabbi Cohen responds. "It contains the fervent prayers of millions of people."

We're speaking to each other on the steps of the Simon Wiesenthal Center Museum of Tolerance. Parishioners from House of Trust and Temple Abraham are here to renew our exchange program. We're visiting the museum as a single unified group.

The modern building on Pico Boulevard stands as a living monument, not only to those who perished in the Holocaust of World War II, but to all victims of bias and hatred. The exhibits are ingenious and painful, especially those that convey the reality of the concentration camps.

The current featured exhibit focuses on the civil rights movement of the sixties. I feel personally involved. A documentary film describes how young people in Birmingham helped bring down segregation by facing very real dangers—dogs and hoses and threats to their lives. We sit and watch in silence. Personal memories flood my mind.

Afterward, Rabbi Cohen tells us, "One of the purposes of this museum is to underscore the notion that bigotry is not restricted to one religion or ethnicity. When prejudice attacks one group—

or one individual—it attacks us all. Facing such prejudice, as these children did, is an act of courage that continues to inspire, forty-five years after the act itself."

We wander around the museum for the next two hours, in groups and individually. By now some of the rabbi's congregants and mine have become friends. We greatly look forward to these get-togethers. Fortunately, the incident with Patrick has been forgiven, if not forgotten.

"Have you seen Patrick recently?" asks Naomi when we sit down for a cup of tea.

"Yes, in fact, he's been a wonderful help to my son, Andre, who has been having some problems."

"Didn't Andre just get married?" she asks.

"I'm afraid that the marriage is the problem."

"I'm so sorry to hear that," says the rabbi. "But I'm glad his cousin is consoling him. Patrick is actually a good listener. Or he can be."

"Patrick is changing," I observe.

"As a result of his move to Fellowship of Faith?"

"Probably," I say, "but I can't be certain because we haven't had that much contact. When we have gotten together, though, he seems much more understanding."

"Maybe he's feeling guilty," says Naomi.

"Maybe, or maybe joining with Bishop Gold is simply good for him. Some people are happier working in larger organizations."

"You can't be happy that he's part of a movement that wants to bury your church under theirs."

" 'Bury' is a harsh word, sweetheart."

"I mean it literally, Albertina. It's such a heavy imposition. And yet I don't see you up in arms."

"These churches have a certain lure. If they didn't, they wouldn't be mega, would they?" I ask.

"Did you happen to hear Roger Stein's special on mega-churches that aired last week?"

"No, I missed it, baby. Was it good?"

"Harshly critical."

"I expected as much. Probably better that I didn't hear it," I say. "By the way, how is Roger?"

"We're not seeing each other anymore."

The statement stops me cold. "I'm sorry," I say.

"No need to be. It just wasn't working."

I want to ask why, but don't. All I say is, "Romantic relationships can be trying."

"Amen. My relationship with God is wonderful, Albertina, but my relationships with men continue to puzzle me."

"I've gone through the same thing," I confess. "In fact, I may still be going through it."

"You're kidding," says Naomi. "You're dating?"

I have to laugh. "Baby, 'dating' isn't a word I'd use. But there are gentlemen who call from time to time. Matter of fact, right now there are two. Now it's down to one."

"Clifford?" she asks.

"Yes, indeed."

"Clifford's a doll," says Naomi. "I knew he was secretly in love with you the moment he met you at my house. I'm glad he found the courage to speak his mind."

"He's quite verbal."

"He's a deejay," Naomi reminds me. "Who's his competitor, Pastor, if I might ask?"

"A fascinating man who's an actor and a cook."

"Great combination."

"And a committed atheist," I add.

"That could be problematic. Do you like him?"

"He intrigues me, darling. But he also exasperates me."

"It sounds like you like him, Albertina."

"I've learned to love everyone in his or her own way."

"A beautiful attitude," Naomi observes.

"Beautiful because the lesson comes from God. But sometimes difficult when you try to apply it to the world of romance."

"Amen, sister," says the rabbi.

Lifetime Achievement

"I can think of no one who deserves this award more," says famed producer Quincy Jones to the throng at the Beverly Hills Hotel. "Clifford Bloom has been an advocate for jazz as America's only original art form. For four decades the man has tirelessly championed the cause of musicians, whether famous or deserving of wider fame. I love him like a brother and am honored to present him with the Lifetime Achievement Award from the Los Angeles Jazz Society. Clifford, you're the best."

The room rises to applause as Clifford walks to the podium. I'm seated at the first table with Clifford's closest friends. The evening has been one long lovefest. Saxophonist Sonny Rollins called Clifford "one of the sweetest cats I know." Pianist Dave Brubeck said, "Back in the dark days of radio, Clifford was programming jazz when no one would dare. He was our champion then, and he's our champion now." Music producer Tommy LiPuma remembered, "If a jazz musician was down and out, Clifford was the first to run a benefit. I don't know how many careers this man has saved. God bless you, Clifford."

Besides the testimonies, there were musical tributes. Oscar Peterson played "You're the Top." Dianne Reeves sang "You Are

So Beautiful." In a surprise appearance, Al Jarreau did a thrilling version of "Thou Swell."

By the time Clifford reaches the podium, I see there are tears in his eyes.

"For a guy who talks for a living," he tells the guests, "this should be easy. When has anyone ever known Clifford Bloom to be at a loss for words? But I'm afraid this is one time that I'm going to have to be brief. No one wants to see a grown man cry like a baby. Let me thank all the wonderful musicians and friends who have spoken and played so beautifully tonight. And let me also express my gratitude not only to them, but to the music that set me on my professional course. Jazz is more than art. To me, it's a reflection of the startling and endless creativity that comes to us as a gift from God. There are so many people I could—and should—publicly thank tonight, but that would take hours. I must, however, acknowledge my friend and pastor Albertina Merci, whose shining example has been a beacon of love."

This is a generous man, I think to myself, *this is a good man*. He has won the respect of his community and the gratitude of his peers. Surely God has placed him in my life for a reason. Surely I am blessed to enjoy his company and this fabulous evening of celebration.

And enjoy it I do. The food is fabulous. I chat with old friends. The Clayton-Hamilton Jazz Orchestra plays a long set of Duke Ellington songs. Diana Krall sings "I'm Beginning to See the Light." Virtually everyone stops by our table to congratulate Clifford on his special night.

We don't leave until eleven-thirty. As we are headed out the door, I glance over to a table in the back and see Mario and Rita Richardson. Mr. Mario looks especially handsome in his tux. Councilwoman Richardson, who is slightly overweight, is nonetheless wearing a form-fitting dark green gown.

They rise to greet us cordially.

"Great evening, Clifford," says Mario. "You deserve all those accolades."

"Thank you, Mario," says Clifford. "I appreciate that."

"And we both appreciate that foxy pastor of yours," adds Mario with a smile on his face.

Love Field

Andre sits beside me on the Southwest Airlines flight to Dallas. It's a Thursday, two weeks before Christmas, and he's going to meet Patrick who has returned to his office at the Fellowship of Faith. He'll be staying at Patrick's apartment, which is close to the church, and meeting with Solomon and Bishop Henry Gold about a writing program. The program has expanded beyond creative writing; they're exploring how, if Andre is hired, he could lead a task force on community-wide literacy. Because public school education is so lacking, students' writing skills are insufficient on almost every level. Patrick has convinced Andre that addressing that problem is something that could give Andre's life—and the lives of others—new meaning.

I can only applaud the effort. Ever since he arrived from New York and began conferring with his cousin, Andre's depression has decreased. He's not back to the old Andre, but he is moving forward. I thank God for that. I thank God for Patrick's plan for his cousin. I have no such plan to offer my son, although I wish I did.

I'm flying to Dallas on the behest of the Davids. I've accepted their offer to stay with them. They touched me with their invitation and intrigued me with the notion of visiting Mama's old church and the church of my childhood.

As the plane flies over New Mexico, I close my eyes and dream of that church. My mother is there. So is Daddy. Darryl is alive and is preaching in the pulpit. He's praying for sinners everywhere. My brothers are ushers handing out fans, and my husband Arthur is a television cameraman filming the service. But somehow the Church of the Nazarene becomes the Regal Theater in Chicago, where Jackie Wilson is singing with Little Willie John and Clyde McPhatter, friends from my days as a blues artist. Laura and Andre sit on the front row, and I am the emcee. I announce my faith in God and my faith in rhythm and blues. I say that singers are preachers and preachers are singers and everyone stands to welcome my mother, whose hair is piled high like Mahalia Jackson's and who sings in a voice that resembles the great gospel artist Clara Ward.

My mother sings "How We Got Over" and motions me to join her.

Now the Regal has become the House of Trust in Los Angeles, and Clifford Bloom is a cameraman, and Justine is selling beauty supply products up and down the aisles. The women are eager to buy her wares, and I am eager to leave church because I have forgotten my sermon.

"Sing instead," urges someone from the congregation.

I sing Otis Redding's song "Respect," made most famous by Aretha Franklin, and there is great rejoicing and dancing.

I awake when the captain announces we'll be descending into Love Field, the city's original airport situated right in the neighborhood where I was raised and learned to love the Lord. I look over and see that Andre is reading the Bible.

Patrick picks us up at the airport. He drives me over to the Davids' house and is curious about the reason for my trip. I'm a little vague but tell him—truthfully, I believe—that it's all about nostalgia. Of course it's about much more.

Marianne is at home with her babies, Esther and Elizabeth,

and shows me their guest room. Their guest room is my childhood bedroom.

"Would you like to take a little nap?" asks Marianne.

"Yes, baby, I would."

To nap in my childhood bedroom is to delve back into seven decades of dreams. I swim in a sea of dreams.

Lightning and thunder wake me up. A storm is passing over the city. I wash my face and walk to the living room where Esther and Elizabeth are looking out the window.

The rain stops as suddenly as it started, and a rainbow, the most radiant I've ever seen, stretches across the great Texas sky.

The girls are excited. I am too. Marianne suggests that we pray.

"Father God," I say, "your miracles stir us, amaze us, and please us. You are the great painter, the great creator, the great storyteller. May we accept our role in Your story with a humble heart and a grateful soul. Bless these little girls in Your love for them and their love for You. In Jesus' name, Amen."

"I'm going to draw the rainbow," says little Esther. She quickly starts coloring on a big piece of paper. She explains that all the colors are the rainbow and that the gold stripe on top of the page is God who makes the rainbow.

"That's lovely, sweetheart," I say.

"You can have it," offers Esther.

"Oh, thank you, baby. What a wonderful present! I'll cherish it forever."

When Norm arrives home, Esther runs to greet him and Elizabeth starts to giggle when he picks her up. He works as a civil engineer for a firm in Arlington.

Marianne prepares dinner. We say grace and eat quietly. Norm discusses the prospect of a raise and promotion at his job. Marianne tells us that she's thinking about starting up a Web site to sell her handmade baby clothes. They turn to me and ask about my family and my ministry.

I tell them about Andre's new prospects with Fellowship of Faith.

"Bishop Gold's church," says Norm. "It's huge."

"Have you worshiped there?"

"Once."

"Did you like it?" I ask.

"I felt lost. But I know Bishop is doing good things for the community. To me, though, it's more like going to a concert to see a star than communing with a pastor."

"The *Dallas Morning News* said something about him expanding the church to Los Angeles," Marianne mentions. "Do you know anything about that, Pastor?"

"I do, children," I say.

I sigh before I start to explain the situation. Not to do so would be less than candid. They were kind enough to invite me here, and I must be honest enough to explain the full situation. They listen attentively, and when I'm through Marianne says, "It sounds like you love your church in Los Angeles."

"I do, baby," I say.

"But it also sounds like you're feeling pushed out," says Norm. "Maybe that's why the Lord gave us the idea of having you come here. A door closes, a window opens."

"It's all in God's hands," I say. "When I start to worry, I remind myself that it's all going to work out. I remind myself that worrying is an option I can choose to avoid."

"That business with Bishop Gold's church, though, is really an amazing coincidence, Pastor," says Norm. "When we asked you here, we had no idea of what you were going through in Los Angeles."

"Would you like to walk over and see the church now?" asks Marianne. "They're having Bible class, but I don't think they'd mind if we dropped in. It's just around the corner."

"Yes," I say, "I'm eager to see the Church of the Nazarene. To tell the truth, I've been dreaming about it."

The church stands on Cedar Springs Road. It's roughly the size of House of Trust, a modest brick building, neatly maintained, with a freshly painted white cross out front. Under the glow of a full December moon, it is luminous. Glorious.

We enter the sanctuary. The pews are the same. The cross behind the pulpit is the same. The smells are the same. I close my eyes and breathe in. I'm flooded with memories. A small group of people in their twenties and thirties sit on the first couple of rows and take notes as a woman, also in her thirties, discusses the Eighty-third Psalm in which God is beseeched to destroy Israel's enemies.

"That's Pastor Cindy Barnes," says Marianne. "She's still in seminary."

Cindy is the name of my niece who died here in Dallas last year. We sit for a while.

"Would you like to meet Pastor Barnes?" asks Norm.

"Let's not disturb her teaching. I'll meet her Sunday."

I'm scheduled to give a guest sermon Sunday.

Andre calls on Saturday to invite me to meet with him, Patrick, and Bishop Gold at the Fellowship of Faith in Oak Cliff. That's the church where my niece Cindy was eulogized during a memorial service. I wonder if Patrick and Bishop have recruited my son to try to convince me to approve their building program.

"Please give my regards to Bishop," I say, "but I think I'll pass on the meeting."

"It's just a discussion of this literacy program they're having me form, and how your church can get involved, Mama."

"That sounds good, son, but we can discuss it when we get home."

That night little Elizabeth wakes up at four a.m. She's screaming at the top of her lungs. When I walk into the living room to see what's wrong, Marianne is holding Elizabeth, trying to comfort the child. Elizabeth is inconsolable.

"Sorry she woke you up," Marianne asks. "Poor baby won't stop crying."

"Probably a bad dream," I say.

"Would you mind holding her for a couple of minutes while I get her teddy bear?"

"I'd love to."

I take the child in my arms. She feels like heaven. I sit with her in the rocking chair. After a few seconds, she stops crying. Perhaps it's the rocking motion or perhaps the novelty of being held by another person.

"You've done it," says Marianne, returning with a teddy bear.

"We'll just sit here for a while, if you don't mind," I say. "This is doing me good."

I close my eyes. Elizabeth closes hers. I sing her a song about the Lord that my mother taught me. In a couple of minutes, the child falls asleep.

"My mother," I tell the congregation Sunday morning, "took me to this church when I was a child. Looking around this wonderful old building, I can't help but think about my mother. The first time I saw Jesus was in my mother's eyes. The first time I understood the power of Jesus was when I understood the story of my mother's life. She started out as a sharecropper in the backwoods of East Texas. Her mother had been a slave in Alabama. She never knew her daddy because he had been sold to another plantation just after she was born. She lost two brothers and a sister to childhood diseases. The white doctors just threw up their hands and let her siblings die. They were never even sent to a hospital. Mama had every reason to hate the world and rail against its injustice. Yet she was filled with love.

"Her love brought her here to Dallas where she met my daddy and they both worked hard to get by. Her love had her hating nobody. Her love had her praising the Lord every day—and I mean every single day—for staying by her side. 'Might not be where I want to be,' Mama would say, 'but I'm not where I was. Glory to God!' She gave God the glory for all things. And she gave us a love and a hope and a feeling for the future that today lets me lead my life in peace.

"Women of my mama's generation were something else. They understood how you can claim victory in the midst of struggle. They understood how no struggle is too great when we work with God. Mama told me, 'Some people would say I had nothing when I was a little girl, but when I had nothing I still had everything. I had God.' That kind of courage is wisdom. And that kind of wisdom is strength. And the combination of courage, wisdom, and strength is something no enemy can deter. You got that combination inside you. Christ put it there. Feel it now! Let it lift your spirit and sing to your heart! Let it change your life from down to up, from negative to positive, from despair to joy, from dark to light!

"So thank you, Mama. I'm feeling you right here and right now. Thank you for taking me to this blessed church and thank this blessed church for having me back for this beautiful reunion. In Jesus' name, let the church say Amen."

Afterward it was old home week. Several of the older people remembered me and my folks. I was surprised by how many faces I recognized and how many names I remembered.

"Pastor," says an elderly woman whose hands have a slight tremble, "I loved what you said and I hope you'll be ministering here personally."

Several others make the same comment.

"No doubt," says Norm when we got back to the David house, "you won them over."

"You won *us* over the minute we met you, Pastor," says Marianne. "Is there any chance at all that you'll come here?"

I don't know what to say.

"I know it's a hard decision," says Norm, "and I also know that a poor church like ours couldn't offer you much, but I have a feeling we would grow with you as our minister. I know you could change lives here."

I thank them for their kind words. Esther asks me to read her a book before lunch, and I'm delighted to oblige her. The book is about how Jesus loves children. After lunch, I'm tired. I always look forward to a Sunday afternoon nap.

"Would you mind if I retired for an hour or two?" I ask my hosts.

"Not in the least," says Marianne.

My sleep is dreamless, and when I awake it's half past three. I decide to check my answering machine in L.A.

Clifford Bloom has called. I told him that I'd be out of town for the weekend but didn't tell him where I was going.

"This is important, Albertina," he says, "so when you have a chance, please give me a call."

I call him, still not revealing my whereabouts.

"Something has come up," he says. "I'd very much like your counsel. It involves my work and would require that I move out of Los Angeles. The idea of leaving your church and leaving you, Albertina, is extremely painful to even consider. But this is a spectacular offer. It's the perfect job for me. I've been asked to head a jazz studies department at a major university."

"Which university?" I ask.

"The University of Dallas."

"Hawaiian Love Song"

"Don't you think he sings beautifully?" asks Justine.

"I do," I say.

"He's a gorgeous man, isn't he?"

"He has an expressive face."

"There's something about Hawaiian men," Justine sighs. "When they smile, I melt. And when this brother sings, I'm sugar on the floor."

Justine and I are sitting on the patio of the Halekulani Hotel on Waikiki Beach. The sun is setting and the sky is a dazzling mixture of hot pink and burnt orange. The breeze is delightful and my lemonade is as good as any I've ever tasted. The fresh pineapple is sweet. The mood is serene. I'm thinking that I was right to accept Justine's kind invitation to join her for a post-Christmas vacation in Hawaii.

I have told Bishop Gold that by the first week in January I will make my final decision about allowing their church construction to go forward.

"You need to get away from all that mess," said Justine, when she asked me to come with her to Hawaii. "I've got this great deal at this luxury hotel."

"I'm surprised you haven't invited Clarence Withers."

"That's just it," she said, "I need to get away from that man.

He's putting pressure on me that I don't need. You and me, Tina, we got pressure from all sides. Hawaii is the place where all the pressure just disappears. Besides, when you think of the health problems we've had this year and the way we've overcome them—"

"The way God has blessed us," I say.

"However it works, we're okay, and we need to celebrate by indulging ourselves. You'll love the spa at the Halekulani. You'll love everything about the hotel."

I do. There's nothing not to love. A morning massage has me feeling ten years younger. An afternoon dip in the ocean is refreshing and cool. And now, sitting on the patio and watching day turn to night, I have to admit that Justine's right. I needed this.

The singer who has got Justine all excited is through performing and is headed straight to our table.

Watch out.

"Ladies," he says in a charming island accent, "I hope you enjoyed the music."

"Loved it," says Justine. She introduces herself before introducing me as *Pastor* Merci.

"Pastor is here to appreciate nature," Justine adds. "I'm here to appreciate handsome Hawaiian men like you."

Even after all these years, I can't get used to Justine's approach to the opposite sex. She doesn't believe in embarrassment, but I get embarrassed for her.

They go on chatting. His name is Ken Kawika. He has CDs for sale. Justine buys two.

"I can listen to it up in my room," she says, "or you can sing to me yourself—up in my room."

"Justine!" I can't help but protest.

"I'm flattered," says Ken Kawika. "And I'd love to invite you both to hear me tonight at ten o'clock. I'll be singing in a club on Kalakaua Avenue, just a few blocks away. If I give you the address, would you do me the honor of attending?"

"I'll be there," says Justine.

"I'm afraid that's past my bedtime," I say, "but thank you anyway."

Over dinner, Justine can speak of nothing else.

"He's a doll," she says, "and you can tell he's a kind and good man."

"*How* can you tell?" I ask.

"His eyes. The eyes are the windows to the soul. His eyes are sweet."

"You have great confidence in your snap judgments, Justine."

"Are you trying to remind me that my judgment in the past hasn't always been so good?"

"You said it, baby, I didn't."

"Anyway, I'm not talking about sleeping with him—"

"You just invited him to your bedroom."

"Oh, I was just talking," says Justine.

I raise my eyebrows.

"You think I was serious?" she asks.

I raise my eyebrows a little higher.

"Albertina, you know me too well."

Dinner arrives. Fresh fish and luscious vegetables. I'm drinking water. Justine's drinking wine.

"What about *your* romantic situation?" she asks.

"I wouldn't use the word 'romantic.' "

"Mr. Mario still missing in action?"

"He has developed a friendship with Councilwoman Rita Richardson."

"When did this happen?"

"Last few weeks."

"That's just to make you jealous."

"I doubt that."

"What about Clifford?"

"He couldn't be more attentive."

"And what about that rich Bishop coming to take over your church?"

"Not worried about it, Justine. I'm resigned to the fact that God's wisdom will be manifest. Making matters even more interesting, though, I've been offered a position in Dallas."

For the first time, I tell Justine about the coincidence: my job offer and Clifford's, both in the same city.

She reacts with surprise, but also enthusiasm. "I'd hate for you to leave L.A.," she says. "I can't imagine living my life without you as my neighbor, but seems like House of Trust isn't trusting you the way it should. Those people got snowed by that fancy preacher with his fancy plans. Maybe going back to your roots might make life easier. Especially if you marry that disc jockey man."

"Who's talking about marriage?" I ask.

"No doubt that's what he wants. Same as Mario. You got your choice, baby. Who do you think would be better in bed?"

"Please, Justine."

"Face it, Albertina. Most of the reasons marriages last have to do with sex. You've been married enough times to know I'm right."

I have to laugh.

"Enough chitchat. I have to go to that club to see Ken Kawika," says Justine. "Are you with me, girlfriend?"

"I'm always with you, Justine, but tonight I'm going to pass. Besides, I have a feeling I'd just be extra baggage."

The trade winds blowing through the open shutters have me sleeping like a baby. No dreams, no anxiety. I wake up early and spend time with the Word. I'm preparing a new series of Bible classes on the parables of Jesus. I love them all—the lost sheep, the lost coin, the lost son. The stories deepen over the years.

Their wisdom is ancient, yet forever new: God is constant; God's arms are open to everyone; it's never too late to come home to God.

When I arrive at breakfast, Justine isn't there. She probably stayed out late. After eating, I sit under the shade and continue reading in the Book of Luke. It's seventy-one degrees, a perfect morning, a cloudless sky. By eleven, Justine still hasn't shown up. I start to worry a bit. At noon I call her room. No answer.

I take a long walk in the afternoon and prayerfully consider my situation. I thank God for all the wonder in my life. I thank Him for introducing me to the Davids and reconnecting me to my past. What a gift to stand in my mother's church and praise His holy name! I thank Him for Clifford Bloom's care and concern for me. He is such a good man with such a good heart. I thank the Lord for uniting Patrick and Andre. Every time I speak with my son, he seems more centered, less afraid, newly revitalized to do good work. Rather than write movies filled with violence and sex, he is now moved to give people the skills that will lead to greater literacy and creativity.

When I get back to my room the phone's ringing. It's Justine.

"He's the one," she says.

"Are we talking about Jesus?"

"Don't be funny. We're talking about Ken Kawika. He's the one."

"Where are you, baby?"

"At Ken's. He has a beautiful house in Kahala. It's a ritzy suburb just outside town. He's right on the ocean. The man is amazing."

"I'm glad you've made a new friend, sweetheart."

"More than a friend, Tina. I'm telling you, he's the one. He said he's been waiting for a woman like me to come along."

"I see," I say.

"You sound skeptical."

"Not at all. I'm just enjoying my vacation, baby, and I'm glad you're enjoying yours."

"I want you to meet him."

"I already have," I say.

"No, I mean *really* meet him. He wants to cook for us tomorrow night. Are you willing?"

I hesitate for a second before saying, "Why not?"

Ken's home is lovely. It sits on a cliff. It isn't large, but it's cozy and tastefully decorated. Ken cooks dinner—no cook, no maid—and serves us himself. The grilled ahi is delicious. He's a man who likes to attend to his guests. As far as I can see, he's a good guy. He asks me many questions about my life. Unlike most men, he doesn't seem to be self-obsessed. He works as a singer all over the islands. He supports himself handsomely. His wife died five years ago. She managed the Marriott Hotel on Waikiki Beach. There's no doubt he's taken by Justine and she by him. They can't keep their hands off each other.

When it comes time to clean up, he won't allow us to help. He clears the table and stacks the dishwasher himself. He makes us coffee and brings us lemon sorbet. When Justine excuses herself and goes to the bathroom, he turns to me and says, "I can't tell you how much I love that woman. She's the answer to my prayers."

The next day Justine shows up at lunch.

"I'm staying on the island," she says.

"You're *what*?" I ask.

"I'm staying in Hawaii. I'm not going back to L.A."

"Justine—" I start to protest.

"Hear me out. I met Ken's brother and sister-in-law last night. She's a sister from Atlanta. These men love sisters. The brother is the merchandise manager at Wal-Mart, right here in Honolulu. When he heard about my position at Target, he offered me a job. Said they actually need someone with my experience. Said I'd fit in perfectly. It's all falling perfectly into place. Look, Tina, I didn't plan this. I didn't set out to meet a man who makes love like someone half his age. I didn't have my sights set on hooking up with a Hawaiian singer who loves nothing more than bringing me breakfast in bed. This man had to be sent by God. I know it. He knows it. Even you must know it. It's too perfect to pass up. And I ain't passing it up. He's asked me to move in."

"After just three days of knowing him?"

"I feel like I've known him my whole life. I'm a hundred percent convinced my prayers have been answered."

"I didn't know you did that much praying, Justine."

"Well, I'm starting now. I hate to leave you, Tina, but I know you'll be coming out here to visit me."

"I must say, baby, this is awfully sudden."

"If you ask a hundred people where they'd rather live—South Central L.A. or on the beach in Hawaii—all hundred people are going to say Hawaii."

I don't have an answer for that.

"Our lives are changing, Albertina," adds Justine. "It's in the cards. I'm moving to paradise. And you're probably moving to Dallas. That's not paradise, but that's your sure-enough home. And the idea that Clifford is also moving there has to tell you something. Why fight it, Tina? Change is an exciting thing. At our age, we're lucky to have this kind of excitement. I'm not about to pass it up. And neither should you."

"What Are You Doing New Year's Eve?"

When I was a young woman, like many young women I wanted a date on New Year's Eve. I didn't want to stay home with my parents. I didn't want to feel left out. I wanted to go where there was excitement and fun. Well, sometimes I had a date and sometimes I didn't. Sometimes I felt lonely and later I learned that I could feel even lonelier when I was actually out on a date.

Either way, New Year's Eve makes me reminisce. This New Year's Eve I'm content to be alone. Clifford invited me to dinner but I politely declined. We had a lovely church service at eight, thanking God for another good year and an even better year to come, and that was enough. I came home and put on Nancy Wilson singing "What Are You Doing New Year's Eve?" remembering how Clifford took me to a Nancy Wilson concert and how much I enjoyed it.

Now I'm enjoying my solitude, looking through the notes on my Restoration Bible, when the phone rings.

"Don't get excited," says Mr. Mario.

"Why would I get excited?" I ask.

"The very sound of my voice excites a lot of people."

I laugh.

"You laughing at me or with me?" he asks.

"Both."

" 'With mirth and laughter,' Shakespeare wrote in the *Merchant of Venice*, 'let old wrinkles come, And let my liver rather heat with wine than my heart cool with mortifying groans.' "

"Are you drunk, Mario?"

"Not in the least, madam. I am merely accepting my fate as a man who sits alone on a lovely New Year's Eve."

"I would have thought that Councilwoman Richardson would be with you."

"No, despite her kind advances, I have backed off. In the end, she and I enjoy a platonic friendship that I'd call superficial at best."

"So tonight you prefer to be alone," I say.

"I'd prefer to be with you."

"Why, thank you, Mario."

"I hope your solitude is not getting you down," he says.

"Not at all. I'm enjoying the pleasure of God's company."

"Why does He always manage to get in the way of our communication?"

"He's the cause of our communication, Mario."

"So we do have communication."

"How else would you describe a phone call?"

"A message from one friend who misses another," he says. "To say less, Albertina, would be a lie. I miss you."

"I miss you as well, Mario."

"Then there's hope."

"I couldn't live without hope," I reply.

"Hope for us," he says.

"Yes, hope for all of us."

"Must you, my dear pastor, express these emotions in such broad theological terms?"

I laugh again. "That's my nature," I say. "I'm a preacher."

"Why remind me?"

"Only to let you know that I am who I am."

"I recognize that," says Mario.

"Sometimes I wonder."

"Why should you doubt me?" he asks.

"Because I feel you are trying to convert me," I say.

"*Me* convert *you*! I have nothing to convert you to."

"Disbelief."

"I believe in many things, Albertina. I define myself as a believer."

"We must be using different definitions," I say.

"That's where the dictionary comes in handy. I could come over there and bring you mine."

"That's kind of you, Mario, but I have a dictionary of my own."

"A rejection," he sighs.

"Just a fact."

"So this call is fruitless."

"This call is fine," I say. "I appreciate the greeting. I'm grateful that you thought of me. And I like hearing your voice."

"Am I hearing the voice of hope in a strictly personal, nontheological context?"

Now I'm laughing out loud.

"Do I detect scorn?" he asks.

"No," I assure him. "My laughter is a sign of respect for a great performance. By the way, how's your book on nutrition coming along?"

"Splendidly. I'm about through. And that's only the beginning of my plans."

"I'd like to hear more about them."

"You will. But when?"

"Sometime soon, Mario," I assure him.

"Look, Albertina, I don't want to wear you out with this call. I just wanted to say that I care, and I wish you Happy New Year."

"I care too, Mario, and I hope next year brings you everything you want."

"I'm tempted to interpret your last remark in a way that's favorable to me—but I won't. I'll just wish you good night."

"Good night, Mr. Mario. God bless."

New Year's Day.

I have no resolution other than to trust God's will with even deeper conviction.

Clifford has invited me to lunch. He was disappointed that I preferred to be alone on New Year's Eve, but, as always, he was understanding.

It's a gorgeous warm winter day. The sun is radiant, the sky a clear cloudless blue. We drive down to Laguna Beach where, perched above the rocks, a quaint little seafood restaurant overlooks the ocean. We sit outside at a table that overlooks the crashing waves.

The crab salad is flavorful, the ice tea minty, the salmon fresh.

"You know what I want to ask you, Albertina," says Clifford. "You've known for a long time."

"I can guess," I say.

"Let me be plain. I love you with all my heart. I want to marry you."

I stay silent.

"Everything you've told me about this offer to pastor in Dallas makes it seem like our union is inevitable, Albertina. Wouldn't you agree?"

"I'm not certain, Clifford. I can't say for sure."

"You know I'm a patient man."

"Patient and loving both," I say. "You're a wonderful man."

"But not the man you wish to marry?" he asks.

"God will reveal what needs to be revealed," I say. "Right now I have to trust God. I can't rush Him."

Jim Gilliam Park

I t's early morning and my son and I are walking through Jim Gilliam Park, named for a beloved Dodger, located on a hillside just off LaBrea Avenue in the center of the black community. The January sky is clear of smog and the temperature is an ideal seventy-five degrees. L.A. in winter is often ideal.

Andre is surprised at my brisk speed. I remind him that I've been getting up early and doing this for years.

"Nighttime used to be the right time for me when I was singing the blues," I tell him, "but when I got into this church life I discovered the mornings. Now morning is the right time."

"Mom," he said, "I've been wanting to tell you what's been happening with me, Patrick, and the Fellowship of Faith."

"I've been eager to know," I admit.

"I appreciate how you've stayed out of this, Mom. I know it hasn't been easy for you."

"I really wanted to pry," I confess. "All mothers want to pry. But I was just happy you were connecting with someone."

We come to a section of the path that faces downtown, off in the distance. The skyscrapers glitter in the sun. A news helicopter hovers overhead. We keep walking.

"At first I didn't even want to talk to Patrick," says Andre.

"That's how angry I was at him. I felt like he'd let you down. I asked him how in God's name could he run off on you like that."

"I didn't take it personally," I say.

"I know that, Mom, but I was still mad. But when he told me that it really wasn't about you, but your church's connection to Naomi Cohen's synagogue, I began to understand. Patrick really opened up to me. As hard as I was hit by Nina, Patrick was hit harder by his thing for the rabbi. I mean, the boy has it bad. I spent days just listening to him. I've never seen anyone so obsessed. He just went on and on. And the strange part was that the more I listened, the more I was able to get out of myself. For the first time since Nina had run off, I could concentrate on someone else's heartache. That gave me relief."

"Did you give him advice, son?" I ask.

"I told him that a love so strong has to be dealt with. He has to find a way to express it. He has to tell her."

"Knowing Naomi, I think she'd be responsive."

"I believe you. But the whole thing frightens Patrick, Mom. That's why he ran off to Dallas and threw himself into Fellowship of Faith. A major distraction. And a way to keep from going crazy."

"Has it worked that way for you as well, Andre?" I ask.

"I think it has. I feel bad about working for a church that is overshadowing yours, Mom, but their writing program really is a good thing."

"I have no doubt."

"It's big and ambitious and something I can really get behind."

"I think that's wonderful."

"So you don't feel like I've betrayed you?"

"Not in the least. God is sovereign. God is in charge of our stories."

"And do you think God is prompting you to go back home to Dallas?" my son asks.

"The experience of preaching in Mama's church was very powerful, Andre. Very moving."

"So you're wanting to move, Mom?"

I stop walking. I feel a little winded. "Mind if we sit for a while?" I ask.

"There's a bench right over there."

We sit.

"Well, Andre," I say. "Here's the situation. I look at my friend Justine. I told you how she met a man in Hawaii and decided to stay. She's coming back next week to pack up and arrange the sale of her house—and that's it. She up and quit her job. She turned her life on its head, just like that."

"And that's appealing to you?"

"I can relax in the knowledge that, one way or the other, God's will *will* be done."

"I always wonder why God so frequently makes His will unclear. Why is it hidden in ambiguity and nuance? Why doesn't he just announce His will? Why doesn't He make it plain?"

"If he did that," I answer, "life wouldn't be so interesting."

"Well, Mom, it's sure going to be interesting to see how this turns out."

"For the best," I say, "always for the best."

Four Days to Go

It's Monday.

Bishop Gold has called my church office twice. He wants to know when I will give him final permission to start building.

"You'll have my decision by Friday," I say.

"Thank you, Pastor. I have every confidence you'll do the right thing."

"Thank *you*, Bishop. I'm certain I will."

All afternoon long I listen to Justine as I help her pack up her things. The girl's flying high. Her romance is on fire. She's burning up with love for Ken Kawika. She can't wait to get back to Honolulu.

"Just this once, Tina," she says, "let me spell out a few of the details of how this man pleases me."

"Please be general."

"It's all in the specifics. Ken Kawika has studied the female anatomy. He knows how to make a woman scream and holler."

"Have you decided which pieces of furniture you're taking?" I ask.

"Just the small pieces my grandmother gave me. The others I'm donating to your church. Have a yard sale."

"Thanks, Justine, but I'm still not certain about what's happening with the church."

"You're moving, just like I'm moving. You're moving in with Clifford."

"Nothing has been decided."

"No, but it has been decided for you—that's for sure. That megachurch has won the war of coercion. No one can beat back Gold. He's too slick. Besides, it's time all of us got out of Dodge. This neighborhood's been falling apart for years. If the potholes on these cracked streets don't get us, a drive-by will."

"I've never heard you talk this way before, Justine."

"I've never had my eyes open before. Ken has opened my eyes."

"Is there talk of marriage?" I ask.

"I don't want it, and neither does he. I'm just moving in, honey. I'm ready to play house. This girl's happy to play house."

That evening, after hours of packing, we slip out to a Japanese restaurant on Jefferson Boulevard. Justine's still flying high. I've never seen her this excited. And I'm beginning to feel excited for her.

As she describes the new life that awaits her, I pray that it all comes true, that Ken really is a good man who cares about her. I pray that romance for women our age can be real and true. I begin to see how wonderful it is to fall in love, just like that. To pick up and start over, to leave one world and enter another, to reinvent yourself at the drop of a hat. Justine does what she wants to do when she wants to do it. I can't help but be attracted to that trait. She acts on whimsy.

Do I?

Of course I don't.

I can hardly act at all. I'm still weighing my options between going and staying. Staying means holding on to a church I love. Going means embracing a church I will come to love. Does going also mean embracing a man I love?

Three Days to Go

It's Tuesday.

I'm in my church office. The board of trustees has given me its vote of confidence. They've said they're behind me, no matter what the decision might be. Three other parishioners call on the phone to say the same thing. I detect that they still favor the Fellowship of Faith building plan, but in their voices I also hear a deep understanding of my dilemma.

"If you decide you don't want that church," says one parishioner, "we'll rally around you. We love you and don't intend to leave you. And we sure don't want you to leave us."

That almost makes it harder. Were the congregation to say that it's their way or the highway, I might hit the highway to Dallas. I could feel like they're ridding themselves of me. But as the day goes on, the phone keeps ringing, each call saying that my position will be honored, no matter what.

That makes me feel good—and even more undecided.

At two p.m., Naomi Cohen calls.

"Could I drop by around five?" she asks.

"I always love seeing you, sweetheart," I say. "You're my favorite rabbi."

When she arrives, she looks worried. Her eyes are tired and drained.

"What's wrong, baby?" I ask.

"We've been talking."

"You and Patrick?"

"Yes, ma'am."

"Well," I say, "that's not entirely a bad thing."

"He has proposed."

"Lord, have mercy," I say, "that *is* a surprise."

"He said he's tired of fooling around with his feelings. He said he has tried to forget me, tried to bury our relationship in the past, but he can't."

"How did you respond, dear?"

"I confessed to feeling the same. I said I've gone through exactly the same thing. All the while I was dating Roger Stein, it was Patrick I was thinking about. Even dreaming about. I know I sound like a schoolgirl, Pastor, but his sincerity brought out mine. All my feelings came to the surface. I spoke my heart. I told him I loved him."

"Naomi, you two had quite a conversation—"

"And he said the same. Those very words. He proclaimed them. He said them to me, over and again, 'I love you. I love you. I'll always love you.' Soon we were both crying like babies. Then he proposed."

"And did you accept?"

"I couldn't speak."

"Have you accepted since your conversation?"

"I want to. But it seems so absolutely crazy. Yet so absolutely right. I guess that's why I'm here—to ask you, Pastor, whether you think I'm crazy."

"Baby," I say, "you're one of the least crazy people I know."

"I've never felt more confused and more certain, all at once."

"How so?" I ask.

"Certain that I love him, confused over what to do about it."

"Was he calling from Dallas?"

"Yes, he's on his way back to Los Angeles. He says he's bought me a ring. He wants this to happen right away. It's too sudden, isn't it?"

"I don't think the question is timing, sweetheart. You've known each other for some time. The question is whether this is what you want. It is, after all, a lifetime commitment."

"And you're saying it's foolish."

"I'm not saying that at all, Naomi. I'm saying that it's one of the most important decisions you'll ever make."

"I asked Patrick point-blank, 'What about religion?' He answered that since it's religion that has kept us apart, we have to find a way for religion to bring us together. I wanted to know how. He said it's all a question of faith. We both believe in God. We both have faith. He argued that with even greater faith, we would find a faith."

"Did you discuss his verbal assault before you and your congregation?"

"We did. He was genuinely repentant. He asked for forgiveness. His words touched my heart. I forgave him, Pastor. I couldn't help but forgive him."

"That's beautiful, Naomi."

"He arrives at LAX in a few hours. He asked that I pick him up at the airport."

"And you agreed?"

"I did."

We stay silent for a minute or so.

"You think I'm wrong?" Naomi finally asks.

"No, I think there's a momentum here that's quite extraordinary."

"Will you pray for us, Pastor?"

"I'd love to."

Naomi reaches out to take my hand. Her skin is tingling.

"Father God," I pray, "we give our hearts over to You at this moment of excitement and uncertainty. We know that You are the

Great Certainty in our lives, and that Your presence is steady, strong, and forever giving. You give us insight, Father, and You give us courage to face our confusions. We pray for patience, knowing that You are eternally patient with the human elements of our hearts and minds. As our stories get more complex and entangled, Father, we take time now to remember that You are the center of our story. We know that with You in our hearts all conflicts are resolved and all dissension diminished. You satisfy us, Father, with Your grace. You calm us with Your constancy, You breathe us with Your loving life and keep us sane and whole. May we keep You ever present in our thoughts and words as we go forth from here to do Your holy will. Let us live with the mystery of that will, Father, even as we pursue its meaning and allow it to change our hearts and shape our lives. In His name, Amen."

"Amen," echoes Naomi.

She squeezes my hand, kisses me on the cheek, and heads for the airport.

I sit alone and keep praying.

Two Days to Go

It's Wednesday and I'm thinking of Friday.

I'm feeling a powerful momentum. It may be the momentum that was prompting Patrick to contact Naomi. It may be the momentum of God moving in everyone's lives. It may be the momentum of a new year that I know will be unlike any other year of my life.

In late afternoon, Clifford Bloom calls.

"Are you free for dinner?" he asks.

"I am," I answer.

"There's a new fish restaurant downtown. Perhaps we could go there after Bible class."

"Sounds good," I say.

Clifford never misses Bible class. This new year we're studying the parables of Christ. Tonight we focus on the Prodigal Son. I begin by showing a large print of Rembrandt's painting of the parable. It's stunning. The old father receives his lost son, who has squandered his inheritance and come home penniless, with loving forgiveness. The elder son, who has stayed home and worked diligently, looks on with grave reservations. Why should the father be so joyful at the return of a renegade when he, the faithful son, has stayed loyal?

We begin by discussing the nature of radical forgiveness and radical grace.

Among the twenty parishioners in attendance, Clifford speaks first.

"May I speak personally, Pastor?" he asks.

"Of course, Clifford. Speak freely."

"I had a younger brother. His name was Levi. When we were kids, we both worked in Papa's radio repair shop. We were poor and times were tough. Mom took in laundry and Papa worked day and night. When I was fifteen and Levi was thirteen, Levi stole the money Mom and Papa had stored in a tea container, some $500. Then he disappeared. It was a devastating blow. I stayed and had to work twice as hard. Meanwhile, Levi got lost in a life of crime. When he showed up fifteen years later, Papa and Mom had both died. He was broke and desolate. He came to see me because he had nowhere to go. He sought my help. And I, I—"

Clifford loses his composure for a second or two. He chokes on his words and fights back tears.

"I didn't help him," he's finally able to say. "I turned him down. Turned my back on my brother. Told him I couldn't forgive him for what he had done to Papa and Mama. I said, 'You're no longer my brother. To me, you're as good as dead.' Three years later, I got word that Levi had died of an overdose. I didn't even have the decency to pay for his burial. In my heart, he had died long before that. I tell you this story because it still weighs heavy on me. When I hear this parable, I can't help but wish I had known about it while Levi was still alive. Not simply known it, mind you, but absorbed it into my soul. So tonight I ask God's forgiveness for my lack of forgiveness. I pray to receive that spirit of forgiveness for the remainder of the years that God grants me on this earth."

Clifford's stirring testimony inspires others to testify on this parable. A mother talks about an unforgiving aunt. A daughter talks about an unforgiving mother. A sister talks about the sibling rivalry between her and her supersuccessful brother. Christ's astounding story leads to a wealth of tales of suffering. The suffering now seems illuminating. Jesus' parable sheds light on so much in our lives. It's a beautiful lesson and a beautiful Bible class.

Later at dinner, Clifford is still remembering his brother.

"I didn't really know him," he says. "I wish I had."

"I'm sure you do," I add, "but in asking God to forgive us, I also feel we have to forgive ourselves."

"How can I?"

"By modeling God. If His forgiveness seems unreasonable, so does ours. It's a question of accepting the miracle of what some like to call radical grace."

"I'm so grateful for your Bible class, Albertina, and tonight's lesson especially. It's a burden I've carried for so long."

"You're growing in Christ, Clifford."

"I'm also growing in my appreciation and love for you, Albertina."

His words embarrass me. He waits for me to declare my love for him. And I do love him. I love his enthusiasm for the Lord, his devotion to God's Word, his courage to declare himself for Christ.

"I start my new job in Dallas at the end of the month," he says. "I've already found a beautiful two-bedroom, two-bath town house halfway between the university and the Church of the Nazarene. I don't want to take it, though, until you've had a chance to see it—and to make up your mind, of course. If I'm not being too pushy, Albertina, I'd like to ask you how you're leaning."

"Leaning on the Lord."

He laughs and says, "Why did I know you were going to say that?"

"You know me pretty well by now, Clifford."

"Yet I don't know what you're going to do."

"Neither do I—at least not right now."

"Friday is the deadline you gave for yourself," he reminds me.

"Friday is the day after tomorrow."

"I wish I could be responsive, Clifford, I really do. You're a wonderful man and I feel like you deserve an answer."

"Albertina, I have to say that in all honesty I believe Dallas is the answer. All indications point in that direction. When you told me that your childhood church had made you an offer, I knew that Dallas *had* to be right. It's too uncanny to be a coincidence. It's the city of your past and the city of our future. Together. Wouldn't you say so?"

"I'm praying on it, dear Clifford. I'm praying unceasingly."

I'm also dreaming unceasingly.

My dreams are little soap operas. All week I can hardly wait to fall asleep to see what will happen next.

In one dream, Clifford and I are living in Paris where we go to a great cathedral. Bishop Gold is preaching in the cathedral and calls us to the altar to be married. The choir is singing "It's Your Thing," the song made popular by the Isley Brothers.

In another dream, Mr. Mario drives by the house in an enormous truck painted black and gold. When he honks, the horn plays the famous Reverend James Cleveland number "Peace Be Still." I get in the truck and we drive to Las Vegas where my old friend Ray Charles is performing. Ray invites me to the stage to sing "I Can't Stop Loving You." When instead I sing, "I can't stop loving Jesus," Ray smiles that broad smile of his. He invites Mario to the stage to recite the "To be or not to be" speech from *Hamlet*. When Mario starts to recite, his spoken words turn musical. He and Ray sing together and *Hamlet* becomes "Mary Don't You Weep."

I half remember a dream where my children are encouraging me to marry a certain man, but I can't make out the name. I tell them, "David says, 'They that trust in the Lord will be as Mount Zion, which cannot be moved.' " They shout back the name of the man they want me to marry. I still can't understand. I see that all my former husbands are there. They're laughing. They wave to me from their seats in the back of a movie theater. On the screen is a larger-than-life love story. I'm in it. I'm walking down a lonesome street in a big city. The city is deserted. The road leads to the country where the sun is shining and flowers are in bloom. I follow the winding path to a garden where a man is waiting for me. Music is playing. Harps, flutes, violins. I start to cry. The man reaches out his hand. I give him mine. A minister reads from Chapter 13 of Paul's first letter to the Corinthians: "Love is patient, love is kind and is not jealous; love does not brag and is not arrogant, does not act unbecomingly; it does not seek its own, is not provoked, does not take into account a wrong suffered, does not rejoice in unrighteousness, but rejoices with the truth; bears all things, believes all things, hopes all things, endures all things."

These dreams continue when I sleep at night and nap by day. I find them fascinating. I'm tempted to analyze them, discuss them with my friend Florence Ginzburg, but I resist the temptation. Surely I understand what's happening.

There's only one day left.

One Day to Go

As Mama used to say, "It's Thursday all day."

In our little house near Love Field, Thursday meant doing homework early because Thursday night was choir practice. I couldn't wait. I was an eager singer for the Lord. That's where I first felt the joy of God's rhythm. That's the rhythm that moved me then and moves me now.

I feel that rhythm in my spirit when I go to Whole Foods to shop for vegetables. The prices are high but their vegetables are fresh. I feel that rhythm in my spirit when I go to the car wash. My PT Cruiser is crying for a cleaning. Lord knows that I'm feeling that rhythm in my spirit when I go to Blondie's hair salon for a quick cut, wash, and blow-dry. Blondie is blasting the new Donnie McClurkin CD, and all the saints, their hair wet and set in curlers, are singing His praises. I'm still feeling that rhythm when I arrive at church and make sure that arrangements are set for our big meeting tomorrow night.

Life has a rhythm, every day and every season has a rhythm, every hour and every minute has a rhythm. Long as we listen for it. Long as we let it wash over us. Long as we let the Lord lead us to that sanctified syncopation that keeps us in the good groove.

I dine alone. Make myself angel hair pasta with a light tomato sauce. Baby lettuce, fresh cucumbers, carrots, a sprinkle of sprouts.

The phone rings many times. Caller ID tells me who's calling. Clifford. Several parishioners. Clifford again. I decide to let the machine take the messages.

When Naomi Cohen calls, I pick up.

"We've been having many long talks," she says.

"Are they fruitful?"

"We're getting closer."

"That's always a blessing."

"We're down to a single issue that only you can resolve."

"I'll do my best."

"We both want you to marry us."

I pause to catch my breath.

"Are you still there, Pastor?" she asks.

"I'm here, baby."

"Well, are we asking too much?"

"No, sweetheart, I just need to brush these tears away from my eyes."

"Tears of joy?" asks Naomi.

"Tears of complete joy," I say.

"So your answer is yes?"

"Yes, yes, yes. Have you picked a date?"

"Within a few months. We have to tell our folks first. That won't be easy."

"Maybe easier than you expect."

"Either way, I'm finally at peace. And so in love with your nephew I can hardly speak. I held in that love for so long that I didn't realize how good it would feel to let it out and let it live."

"Glory to God," I say.

"Thank you, Albertina. I've been praying for you as well. Praying that you've come to an equally calm decision."

"I've been calm, darling, even relaxed, and I keep thinking that the decision will come with a bolt of lightning—or something or someone will make it for me. So I put it out of my mind and stay in prayer. Tomorrow will come soon enough."

Thursday night, though, sleep doesn't come easily. I toss and turn, my mind going here, going there. I close my eyes and see the giant Fellowship of Faith sanctuary in Dallas. I close my eyes and see the House of Trust, the Church of the Nazarene. I drift in and out of dreams. Clifford is there, Mario disappears, Patrick and Naomi are there, my children, Mario appears, Clifford disappears, they both appear, their faces dissolve, the church organ swells, then fades, then swells.

Stay Out of the Kitchen!

It's Friday and the song says, "It's already here . . . everything that God promised you."

I believe the words. It's already here.

The peace. The victory.

I look forward to my lunch date with Florence Ginzburg.

We meet at an outdoor café in the farmers' market. I recognize an old actor from a TV series that gave me pleasure for many years. He's an invalid but his smile has retained its radiance. I go over and thank him for his beautiful dramatic work. "God bless you," he says.

Florence arrives looking fresh and vital. She's a wellspring of good energy. She wants to hear all about Andre. I tell her the good news, and she's amazed.

"So it's working out," she says.

"Everything usually does."

I tell her the story about Patrick and Naomi.

"That's fantastic, Tina," she says. "There's recovery and reconciliation everywhere we look. You must feel wonderful."

I tell her about tonight's church meeting.

"My God," she says, "and you sit here cool as a cucumber."

"I can't explain it, Florence, but I have this strong feeling that I'll be led in some way that I can't see right now."

"If I were in your position, Tina, I'm not sure I'd have your kind of serenity. Either way, will you call me with the results?"

"Of course I will, sugar."

The rest of the afternoon is quiet. A few calls from curious parishioners who can't wait for tonight and must have advance word. I have none to give. Instead I work on my Sunday sermon, the parable of the Lost Sheep.

At about four o'clock I look out the window and see a stretch limousine pull up to the church. I recognize it as belonging to Bishop Gold. The Bishop himself emerges and heads inside. I expect that he also wants advance word of my decision.

When he reaches my office, though, I see that his demeanor is neither curious nor especially friendly. He is visibly angry.

"I wouldn't have expected this of you, Pastor," he says as he stands before my desk. "To be perfectly honest, I find this maneuver beneath you. I would never have dreamed you'd go to such lengths."

"Please have a seat and tell me what you're talking about, Bishop," I say, "because I really have no idea."

"Don't take me for naïve," he barks back. "I thought we had an understanding. I went to every possible length to accommodate your needs and make sure your church's integrity would be protected. Now this."

"Now what?" I ask.

"And to do it all under the subterfuge of a surrogate."

"Bishop, I really am baffled. What subterfuge are you talking about? What surrogate?"

"What else is this Mr. Mario to you?"

"Mr. Mario?"

"Yes, Mr. Mario. The same man I tried to help with a health book and nutrition plan. I knew he was ambitious and I knew he was important to you. We were careful to make a place for him. But now this last-minute manipulation by the two of you is the last straw. I tried to reason with him but he's absolutely impossible. He claims he's acting alone, but I'm loath to believe that. I see this as your doing, Pastor, not his."

"I have no earthly idea what you're referring to."

"Seeing is believing. Just follow me."

The Bishop turns and walks out of my office. I follow. He walks out the front door of House of Trust, turns to his left, and walks down Adams Boulevard. His limo follows us slowly. He stops in front of the medium-size grocery store ten yards down the street.

"Take a look for yourself."

On the window is a sign. Huge red letters declare:

MR. MARIO'S

Stay Out of the Kitchen

GRAND OPENING OF

HEALTH FOOD CAFÉ

COMING SOON!

"Now tell me," says Bishop, "tell me you knew nothing about this."

"Absolutely nothing," I tell him.

"That's hard to believe, Pastor. It's hard to believe that you had no knowledge of the fact that Mario, behind our backs, outbid our offer to this grocer and bought his business and the land it stands on, thus rendering our block-long building project impossible."

I shake my head with wonder.

"I demand that you reason with this man," Bishop orders.

"Demand?" I say.

"Yes, *demand*."

"Forgive me if I question your authority in this area, Bishop. But if the man owns the building and doesn't want to sell, your demand doesn't mean very much."

"You lacked the courage to declare your unwillingness to sell, so you gave the dirty work to this Mr. Mario. That's it, isn't it?"

"No, it's not, Bishop, and I must say I find your insinuations inappropriate, especially coming from a minister of God."

With that he motions to his driver. The limo pulls up to the curb, the driver gets out and opens the door, and Bishop slips inside. He doesn't even say good-bye.

I stand alone and take another look at the sign. I can't help but smile. Can't help but feel good inside. I see a light inside the store where construction has started. I hear the sound of an electric drill. I look in and see Mr. Mario hard at work. When the drilling stops, I gently tap at the door. He looks up and waves.

"Hi, neighbor," he says.

"Why didn't you tell me?" I ask.

"You didn't ask."

"How could I ask when I didn't know what you were doing?" I say.

"You knew I was planning a health food café. I told you that. I also told you that I see it as a chain that will spread across the country. And they won't be in the suburbs, Albertina. They'll all be in the inner city where they belong."

"And you secured the financing?"

"With the help of some fat cats in the TV business, yes. I'm well financed."

"But why this location?"

"I love Adams Boulevard. And I love being close to you. Besides, I figured you could use a little help beating back the bad guys. I didn't like the way they were pushing you around, so I pushed back."

"I don't know what to say."

"Say what Juliet said to Romeo—'Take all myself.' Say you love me, Albertina, as I love you. Say you'll marry me. Say it right and right here."

I stand there for a few silent seconds.

"I'm grateful to you, Mario. Truly grateful. In my heart, I always wanted to keep my church intact. God has used you to achieve that aim."

"God has nothing to do with it, my dear."

"You are his instrument, Mario."

"If I admit to that false notion, will you marry me?"

I can only laugh.

"Look, Albertina," says a frustrated Mario, "why don't you just admit that I'm the one man fascinating enough and crazy enough to make you happy?"

"I admit that I love you, Mario. But as God is my witness, I cannot marry a man who denies God's very existence."

"I can change you, Albertina, I know I can."

"And that's how I feel about you, Mario."

"So it's a battle of wills?" he states.

"Perhaps so," I say. "Perhaps so."

Acknowledgments

I thank God for allowing me the space and time in this life to do something I never dreamed of doing. I thank Him for the good fortune of being introduced to David Ritz.

I thank my dear mother and father, Mertis and Lillie John, my husband, Sam, my children, Jesse, Joel, Otis, Limuel, Sherry, Paul, Sharon, and John; my grandson, Jesse, and my granddaughter, Jasmine; and a great lady and friend I watched grow up who said, "Mab, you can do this!"—Ms. Susaye Greene. Last but not least, Dr. Charles Queen, my Greek and Hebrew teacher. To God the glory!

—Mable John

Much love and gratitude to my co-author Mable John, whose sweet spirit opened my eyes and my heart; Janet Hill, wonderful editor and creative partner; my forever friend and loving wife, Roberta; my daughters, Alison and Jessica; my sons-in-love, Henry and Jim; my granddaughter, Charlotte Pearl; my grandsons, Alden Bryan and James Emmanuel; my sisters, Elizabeth and Esther; my dad, Milton; my agents, David Vigliano and Mike Harriot; my publisher, Stephen Rubin; and my brothers, Alan Eisenstock, Harry Weinger, and Leo Sacks. Special thanks to Skip Smith, whose contribution to my spiritual life is incalculable.

—David Ritz

Reading Group Companion

1. Is it possible for an atheist and a pastor to have a fruitful romantic relationship? Why or why not?

2. Do you believe either Mario or Clifford would be a suitable partner for Albertina? Why or why not? If you were Albertina, with whom would you have chosen to pursue a romantic relationship? Why? If you were Justine, whom would you suggest Albertina pursue?

3. *"Be ye not unequally yoked together with unbelievers: for what fellowship hath righteousness with unrighteousness? and what communion hath light with darkness?"*
—2 CORINTHIANS 6:14 (King James Version)

What do you take this scripture to mean? How would you use it to advise the various characters in this book: Albertina, Mario, Clifford, Justine, Andre, Nina, Patrick, Naomi?

4. How do Justine and Albertina maintain a friendship when their values seem to differ so greatly? Have you ever considered someone with values opposite to yours to be a best friend? How and why did the relationship work?

5. How do you think Albertina's former marriages are affecting her actions toward the men who are pursuing her now? How do her religious beliefs shape the way she deals with men now?

6. Albertina has serious reservations about Andre's choice of Nina as his soul mate. If you were a mother with reservations about your child's choice in a mate, how candid would you be? How might you address the issue with your own child? Would you have told your son that you suspected his fiancée of cheating if you actually had some evidence that pointed in that direction? Explain.

7. Both Mario and Albertina are concerned about taking care of the body. Mario aims his energy at having people connect with their physical body through food. Albertina wants to nurture the body with spiritual food. In what ways are you connecting with and nurturing your own body?

8. In *Stay Out of the Kitchen* there is also the issue of the body of Christ as acknowledged through the Christian faith versus the antithesis of that embodiment in the practice of Judaism. Can Christians and Jews share a religious relationship despite their polarized views on Jesus Christ? If so, how could that relationship best be supported?

9. "The Messiah we worship . . . wore sandals, rode a donkey, and was homeless. The Messiah we worship talked about the meek inheriting the earth. He warned about losing ourselves in worldly possessions. He kicked the merchants out of the Temple. He died without a single possession." These are the thoughts of Albertina Merci as she observes the activities at the Mega Joy Conference in Dallas. What are your views on the small "mom and pop church" versus the megachurches? Can a church be run like a business and still be true to the work that God intends?

10. If you were searching for a religious institution to join would you look for a small start-up, a small established place of worship, a large established institution, or a megachurch? What are the advantages of one over the other? What about the disadvantages?

11. Albertina Merci lives through prayer. It sustains her through that which is difficult and keeps her grounded and connected when things are going well. Is there anything in your own life that serves a similar purpose? What is it and how has it developed over time?

12. In this book you meet several characters with very distinct personality traits. Are there any traits that stand out as ones you really admire or appreciate in a person? Any characteristics that you cannot tolerate? Which characters in *Stay Out of the Kitchen* would you want to have as a friend? A family member? A colleague? Which character could you imagine being an enemy?

13. Explain your understanding of the title of this book, *Stay Out of the Kitchen*.

14. Predict what will happen between Albertina and Clifford. Predict what will happen between Albertina and Mario. Who are you rooting for?

ABOUT THE AUTHORS

MABLE JOHN is the author of *Sanctified Blues* and was the first female recording artist for Motown, the lead "Raelette" for Ray Charles from 1968 to 1976, and a successful solo artist for Stax/Volt. She's now an ordained minister with a doctorate in counseling. Dr. John will appear in the upcoming John Sayles movie *The Honey Dripper*. She is also featured on the Stax 50th Anniversary Celebration CD boxed set.

DAVID RITZ is the coauthor of *Sanctified Blues* with Dr. Mable John and the author of *Messengers: Portraits of African American Ministers, Evangelists, Gospel Singers, and Other Messengers of the Word*, as well as biographies of Marvin Gaye and jazz singer Jimmy Scott. He has also coauthored autobiographies of Ray Charles, B.B. King, Aretha Franklin, Smokey Robinson, and other musicians. He lives in Los Angeles, California.